Jess and the
Fireplug Caper

The Twelve Candles Club

Jess and the Fireplug Caper

Elaine L. Schulte

BETHANY HOUSE PUBLISHERS
MINNEAPOLIS, MINNESOTA 55438

Published in association with the literary agency of Alive Communications, P.O. Box 49068, Colorado Springs, CO 80949.

Lines from "Wind" are reprinted from *The Poems of Eugene Field*, (New York: Charles Scribner's Sons, 1920).

Published by Bethany House Publishers
A Ministry of Bethany Fellowship, Inc.
6820 Auto Club Road, Minneapolis, Minnesota 55438

Printed in the United States of America

Library of Congress Cataloging-in-Publication Data

Schulte, Elaine L.
    Jess and the fireplug caper / Elaine Schulte
        p. cm. — (The Twelve Candles Club ; bk. 2)
    Summary: While performing as clowns at parties, Jess and the other members of The Twelve Candles Club solve a mystery and rejoice when Jess's dad returns to the faith.

    [1. Mystery and detective stories. 2. Clubs—Fiction. 3. Christian life—Fiction.]
I. Title. II. Series: Schulte, Elaine L. Twelve Candles Club ; bk. 2.
PZ7.S3867Je   1992
[Fic]—dc20   92-15203
                                                                CIP
                                                                AC
ISBN 1-55661-251-6

To

the real Jingles,

the real Officer Drane,

and to Lauren Bullock,

another helper

CHAPTER

1

*O*rder in the court, the monkey wants to speak! Speak, monkey, speak!" the girls chorused outside Jess's door. They laughed hysterically, probably because it was to be their first clowning practice. "Order in the court, the monkey wants to speak—"

Jess McColl, feeling strangely uneasy in her room, was glad to hear her friends. She jumped up from her desk, wearing a red clown suit with white polka dots. "Hold everything!" she called out.

They pounded on the door, and Becky announced in her presidential tone, "Time for the Twelve Candles Club's clowns to come to order."

"To order?" Cara laughed. "Since when has this club ever been in order?"

"Order in the court . . ." they began to chant again. Probably it was one of Tricia's endless wacko sayings.

"Coming! I'm coming!" Jess yelled, nearly tripping over the ankle ruffles on her clown outfit. Finally, she threw open the front door to her bedroom, which was really a converted garage.

There stood her three friends, all neighbors, bouncing with excitement in the southern California sunshine. They wore shorts and T-shirts as usual, and carried their bright yellow and red yarn wigs, and polka-dot clown suits.

"Four-thirty!" Becky Hamilton announced. "Time for the Twelve Candles Club's clowns to come to order."

They trooped in: *Secretary*, Cara Hernandez, a shy girl with big brown eyes in her sweet face and beautiful black hair . . . *Treasurer*, Tricia Bennett, a dramatic green-eyed blondish red-head . . . and *President*, Becky Hamilton, a lanky, aspiring artist with blue eyes and long, dark brown hair. Tricia carried a makeup case, and Cara had a video camera, ready to tape their party-helper clowning acts.

Tricia looked Jess over. "Hey, you look great! All you need is your wig and makeup."

"Didn't want to cut the bangs on my wig till you guys came," Jess explained. "If I cut them too short, there's no way to make them long again."

"I'm having trouble with my ankle ruffles," Cara complained. "Let's try on the suits now, before the phone starts ringing."

As Jess closed her front door, they all heard a loud *clang*, followed by more clanging in the backyard, beneath her window. Jess's hair rose on the back of her neck.

"What's *that?*" Tricia asked, her green eyes huge.

"I don't know," Jess choked out. "We're supposed to be the only ones here."

They all glanced at the back window, where sunshine streamed in through the half-open slats of the mini-blinds.

"I heard noises out there a while ago," Jess whispered, her voice shaky. "I . . . I was trying to ignore them. We'd better look to see if anyone's there, but not let them know we're coming."

"Leave the clown stuff here," Tricia whispered back, dumping hers on the white carpet. "Let's amble to the back window. Pretend we're admiring ourselves in the mirror by your ballet *barre*, then we'll rush to the window and open a slat to peek out. All right?"

Jess nodded, her heart pounding. "Good idea."

"Let's go!" Tricia whispered.

The four of them strolled, stiff-legged, to the back window. "Oh, look at us," Tricia remarked loudly, giving herself a kooky wave in the mirror. "Wow, look at Jess in her red polka-dot clown suit. Isn't she just too much?" Then she hissed under her breath, "Slowly . . . eyes on the mirror, keep acting silly. . . ."

"Silly . . . silly. . . !" Becky croaked.

They were a silly sight, all right, Jess thought, though she couldn't have laughed for anything. Her knees were too weak and her hands were shaking.

"Two more steps to the window," Tricia whispered, then she yelled, "*Now!*"

They yanked back a slat on the mini-blind and peered out.

No one. No one peering in, and no one on the hillside behind the house, either. Only a few bees buzzed over the purple flowers of the ice plant. High above, nothing moved behind the bushes that hid the concrete drainage swale. And it was impossible to see very far to the left because the main part of the house jutted out, and a white stucco wall hid the pool and the patio.

"Maybe it was just a cat knocking over a metal bucket or something," Jess guessed, her knees still weak. She shut the mini-blind as tightly as she could, anyway.

Cara's brown eyes were enormous. "Last night on the TV news they said something about burglaries in Santa Rosita. I think they said the burglar stole a VCR, jewelry, tools, and other stuff."

Becky studied the room from the window. "What would anyone have seen looking in here?"

"First of all, they'd have seen a clown or two," Jess said.

"You wacko!" Becky said. "I meant, what would they have seen to steal?"

Jess looked around her bedroom.

It was a white high-ceilinged room that had once been a three-car garage and now had big front and back windows to let in lots of light. Her front door led out to the front sidewalk, and her side door led into the two-story mid-section of the house. In the corner, the twin beds and table would have been mostly out of sight. But anyone looking in could have seen the white chest of drawers and matching desk, as well as blue floor mats, a small trampoline, a gymnast's beam and vaulting horse, and huge posters of Olympic gymnasts.

Jess shook her head. "I can't imagine anyone wanting to steal my gymnastics equipment. For one thing, it'd be too heavy to carry out, and there certainly aren't many people who'd want it."

"Maybe they'd be interested in your silver trophies," Cara ventured.

Jess looked at the gleaming trophies that lined the shelves

on her side wall. "Why would anyone want trophies with my name engraved on them?" To someone else, they wouldn't mean any more than the photos, newspaper clippings, or prize ribbons on her bulletin board.

"You know how some burglars are," Becky said. "Better phone your mom."

"She's out showing property, and Dad's flying home from Singapore." It was one of those times Jess wished her mother weren't a realtor and her father weren't an airline pilot, even if their jobs did sound exciting.

"What about your brothers?" Tricia asked.

"All three are working."

"Your mom's white Mercedes is in the driveway," Cara said.

"Mom took the Jeep," Jess explained. "She's showing property out in the boonies and needed four-wheel drive."

Tricia lowered her voice. "The thing to do if you're scared is to take the bull by the horns—but carefully."

"Meaning what?" Cara asked, her face pale.

"Meaning we look out again," Tricia answered.

Cara shrunk back. "Again?!"

"Sure," Tricia said. "If anyone's there, they'd feel safe to snoop around with the blind closed. If we see someone, we dial 911."

"You look out the window and I'll dial," Cara said nervously. She hurried to Jess's desk, where a phone hung on the wall.

"Cara Hernandez, you are a chicken!" Tricia told her.

Cara sat down at the desk, raising her chin. "*Someone's* got to call the police."

"All right," Jess whispered, her heart thumping hard. "We

three line up in front of the mini-blind and lift this slat—" she pointed "—on the count of three. Cara, get ready to dial 911."

"I've got my finger on the nine," Cara responded, holding up the receiver for them to see.

"Okay, okay," Jess whispered, her heart still racing. She counted nervously. "One . . . two . . . three!"

They jerked up the slat and peered out the window.

"Nothing!" Jess sighed with relief. A moment later, another thought hit. "Maybe we'd better check the whole house! Tricia, would you . . . would you come with me?"

Tricia rolled her eyes. "If Cara stays by the phone."

"I will," Cara promised. "Believe me, I will!"

Becky hurried to the side door with them, her face pale. "I'll hold the door open, so we can hear if you yell."

"Good idea," Jess told her, then swallowed hard. "Shhh! We'd better be quiet." She swallowed again as she started through the side door to the laundry room and kitchen. She whispered to Tricia, "Let's check all the doors and windows."

The laundry room and kitchen were empty. No problems there. The cleaning lady had been in this morning, and everything looked neat and clean. Except for Jess's room, the entire house was decorated in a sleek southwestern style—white, tan, salmon and turquoise—as if they lived in New Mexico instead of southern California.

They tiptoed through the family room, and Jess peered out the sliding glass door. Outside, the patio, pool, and back hill were perfectly still. She tugged at the sliding glass door. "Locked," she whispered, her mouth dry. "Let's check the front door."

They snuck out from behind the spiral staircase and headed for the front door. Jess tried the knob. Locked.

They walked quietly through the dining room and living room. Everything was in order.

"What about upstairs?" Tricia whispered.

The upstairs had a guest bedroom, her parents' master suite, and Dad's office. *Maybe* . . . Jess thought. Then glancing up, she could see that no one had been there since noon. "The cleaning woman vacuumed the stairs this morning, and there's not a fresh footprint on the carpet. That leaves only my brother's rooms." She eyed the white carpeting that led to their end of the house. "No footprints there, either. Only vacuum cleaner marks."

Tricia raised an eyebrow. "Good detective work, Jess. Who else would think to look for footprints on the carpet?"

"Only because Mom *hates* footprints on the carpet so much," Jess answered, beginning to relax.

On the way back, they checked the kitchen and family room windows, but everything was locked.

Becky still stood with the door open when Jess and Tricia returned. "What's up?"

Jess shook her head. "Nothing. No problems. You can hang up the phone, Cara."

"Whew!" Cara said, replacing the receiver.

Becky flopped down on one of the beds, flinging her legs up and letting them fall again with a thump. "Double whew! If someone *was* there, we probably scared them away when we were laughing about clown practice. And if anyone strange was lurking around the bushes by the drainage swale, I think we would have noticed when we crossed the street from Cara's house."

"I didn't look there," Cara said, rising from the desk chair. "We were all busy talking and laughing."

15

"I didn't either," Tricia admitted.

Becky pursed her lips, thinking. "I'm not sure if I did, but your house is only one story high where your room and the new garage are, so we had full view of the hill out back. Even if we weren't looking for trouble, we'd have noticed any movement back there."

"The wind must have blown over a bucket or something," Jess decided, even though it wasn't windy outside. "Who cares, anyhow!"

"Yeh!" Becky said. "So let's clown it up, clowns! Mom says the kids will pay a lot more attention to us if we're dressed up like clowns."

"Let's hope so," Cara commented. "I can't handle another party like Staci Thurston's, with the whole kindergarten class out of control."

"You know it," Jess agreed. She felt better, but still not quite right about the noise they'd heard outside. The thought of someone lurking around the house made her feel creepy.

Cara, Becky, and Tricia pulled on the colorful polka-dot clown suits over their shorts and T-shirts. It was a good thing Tricia's mother knew how to make costumes. Yesterday, they'd all helped her with the baggy clown outfits and the yarn wigs. Now all they had to do was cut the wigs into the lengths and shapes they wanted and arrange the neck ruffles.

"These outfits are great!" Becky enthused. "Can you snap me up?" she said to Jess.

After a moment, they were all snapped up into the baggy outfits, fluffing and arranging the bright ruffles around their faces.

"Whoa, check us out in the mirror!" Tricia said.

They all faced the big mirror behind the ballet *barre*. "It doesn't even look like us!" Jess exclaimed.

"Wacko!" Becky declared. "The Twelve Candles Club moves into the clowning business." She wore a blue clown suit, as bright blue as her eyes. Tall and lanky, she was the tallest clown and a little klutzy. She took off her white headband to try on her wig.

Tricia and Becky knew about clowning, since they'd taken a class. Now Tricia lifted her reddish hair from the shoulders of her green polka-dot clown suit. "Pin up your hair. There are extra hairpins in the makeup case."

Jess eyed herself in the mirror as she pinned up her light brown hair. When she put on the red yarn wig, the bangs hung almost to her nose. "Hey, check this out. I'm taller with the wig," she told the others. "Either that, or I'm finally growing!"

"You're the perfect size for a gymnast," Cara said, "short and compact." She gave each foot a little kick, trying to adjust the leg ruffles.

"Just call me Fireplug," Jess said, "*short* for fire hydrant."

"Fireplug! That's a great clown name for you!" Tricia exclaimed.

"Especially in a red clown outfit, right?" Jess added. "Hey, we all need clown names. How about the rest of you?"

They studied themselves in the mirror, trying to think of the right names.

Tricia cocked her yellow raggedy head thoughtfully. "Jingles," she decided. "I want to be called Jingles. I'll wear little bells on my tennies and wrist ruffles."

"Then Jingles you are!" Jess announced. "How about you, Beck?"

Becky stared into the mirror. "Beck-o, I guess. Besides, I can't think of anything else."

17

Tricia jumped up like a cheerleader. "Hurray for Beck-o!"

"Cara?" Jess asked.

Cara rolled her brown eyes. "Lello, I think."

"*Lello?*" Jess repeated.

Cara laughed. "Yeh. Because of my yellow clown suit and yellow wig, and my little cousin says *lello* for yellow."

Jess stretched out an "Oh-h-h." Then, grinning, she announced, "Ladies and gentlemen, meet Jingles, Beck-o, Lello, and Fireplug! Now, we'd better do some routines to see if we can really pull off these clowning acts."

"Don't forget, we have to stay close to the phone in case we get calls for jobs," Becky reminded them, being presidential again.

"Something's wrong with my ankle ruffles," Cara said. "Look how they twist around."

Becky fussed with Cara's ruffles, twisting them one way and then another, but nothing helped.

"Why don't I try on your outfit, Becky," Cara suggested. "Your ankle ruffles are perfect. Maybe I can figure out what's wrong with mine."

They both took off the outfits, and Cara pulled on Becky's. It hung in huge folds around her ankles. "Whoa, this is enormous!"

"Well, I *am* tall," Becky reminded her. "Besides, yours is small." She began to try on Cara's, and the ankle ruffles came almost up to her knees. "Yipes! I can't get both shoulders in. I'm stuck!"

"Don't tear it, whatever you do!" Cara yelled.

"I won't!" Becky answered, still struggling. "I'll just take my time getting it off. After all, I got in this far—"

Just then the phone rang, and Cara, who was closest to it,

grabbed it. "Twelve Candles Club." She sat down at the desk. "There are four of us, and we're all twelve years old. We do light housecleaning, car and window washing, baby-sitting, and party helping, which now includes clown entertainment for kids' birthday parties. We also have Morning Fun for Kids, a daycare for kids four to eight years old on Monday, Wednesday, and Friday mornings."

Jess was just thinking that their new greenboard over her desk already showed a busy week ahead when Cara's tone turned peculiar. "Hel-lo," she said. "Hello? Hello?" She replaced the receiver, looking puzzled. "They just hung up."

"Hung up?" Jess repeated, plopping down beside Becky on one of the beds. "What did they say?"

"Nothing, really. A man just asked what the Twelve Candles Club was. I told him—you heard me—" Her eyes widened. "Then he hung up. You don't suppose he had anything to do with . . . the noise we heard outside. . . ." She pointed toward the window.

Jess shook her head. "We were really careful who we gave the flyers to, so we wouldn't get any weirdos calling."

"But there *was* all of that TV and newspaper publicity," Becky reminded them.

Jess nodded. She thought of Becky and the crazy dog chase up Ocean Avenue. It had been shown over and over on the TV news. Later, she'd been interviewed on Channel 10 and told about the purpose of the Twelve Candles Club. "They could have gotten my phone number from your TV interview when you gave it out."

"I guess so," Becky said, looking remorseful. One shoulder still stuck out of Cara's yellow clown suit, but she acted as if she'd forgotten it.

"I suppose it could have been a random caller who just happened to hit this number," Tricia said. "Or maybe a client interrupted by a doorbell. They'll probably just call back."

They all jumped when the phone rang again.

Cara stared at it, her brown eyes wider than ever.

"I'll get it," Jess said, grabbing the receiver. "Hello, Twelve Candles Club." She listened as the phone went dead, then hung up herself. Chills rushed up and down her spine. "It's a phantom caller, all right."

"What should we do?" Becky asked.

"You tell us," Jess croaked, "you're the president."

Becky drew a deep breath. "If it keeps up, we'll have to call the phone company. Gram got some weird calls, and they gave her a new phone number."

Cara shook her head. "But our clients already know this number—" The phone rang again, and she backed away, almost tripping over the big folds of Becky's blue suit around her ankles.

Becky picked up the phone and answered steadily, "Twelve Candles Club. May I help you?" Then she smiled. "Yes, Mrs. Llewellyn, we have you scheduled for housecleaning on Thursday morning. A small dinner party on Friday night? I'll have to ask the others and call you back. Oh, all right—"

Becky put her hand over the receiver. "She wants two people for Friday night, and she wants to know *now*. Who can work from six to ten Friday?"

Jess put her hand up.

"I can do it too," Becky said.

Tricia groaned. "I have to go to Los Angeles and stay with my father, otherwise I would."

"I'm going to L.A., too," Cara added.

Becky nodded and spoke again to Mrs. Llewellyn. "Jess and I can work from six to ten Friday night . . . don't worry, we won't forget. Cara will write it down on our greenboard."

Cara leaned over in Becky's blue clown suit to chalk the job up on their new board. Under Friday, she lettered:

> Jess/Becky,
> party helpers,
> Mrs. L.,
> 6 to 10 p.m.

"Do you want us to wear the cowgirl boots again?" Becky asked. Then looking down at Cara's ridiculously small clown suit she was half-wearing, she added, "We have clown outfits now, too. . . . Oh, a more formal party? Okay. White skirts and blouses. Great. Thank you, Mrs. Llewellyn—"

"Ask if she called earlier," Jess prompted.

"Ahh . . . you didn't call a few minutes ago and hang up again, did you?" Becky asked. "Oh. Well, thanks. It must have been someone else. See you Thursday morning."

As soon as Becky hung up, the phone rang again. She raised her dark brows and picked it up. "Twelve Candles Club. Oh, hello, Mrs. Terhune. How's your new baby?" Before Becky was finished talking, she and Jess were scheduled to clean house for the Terhunes on Saturday afternoon. She hadn't called earlier, either.

Cara chalked the details on the greenboard, and Jess made some notes in her new daily-planner calendar. They all decided there probably had been no one outside the window, and the phantom calls had been someone's dialing mistakes.

After that, the phone rang steadily with one job after another. None of their clients said they'd phoned earlier.

At precisely 5:15, Mrs. Davis called to make sure they'd be there tomorrow in their clown outfits for her twins' birthday party. It had been her idea that they try clown suits. It seemed to all of them like a good way to get more birthday party helper jobs by telling people that they could dress as clowns.

After the calls tapered off, Tricia opened her plastic bag. "I almost forgot! I brought my new white dress shoes to show you. Mom let me get one-inch heels, since I bought them with my own money." She put one on and stretched out her foot to show the others the patent leather pump with dainty satin bow.

Jess admired it, then turned everyone's mind back to club business. "Looks like a busy week ahead. Tomorrow morning there's housecleaning again for Mrs. O'Lone. We'd better be on our bikes by 8:30. Remember, it takes twenty minutes—"

Suddenly Mom's car horn alarm began to blast from the driveway. HONK . . . HONK . . . HONK . . . HONK. . . .

Jess leaped up and ran to the front window, almost tripping over her ankle ruffles. Mom's car stood in the driveway, but no one was near it. Then she heard the sound of a car door slamming down by the street, but it was hidden by bushes.

The car's motor sputtered to life as the alarm on Mrs. McColl's car honked on and on. "They're driving away!" Jess yelled, every muscle tensed.

"Call the police!" Cara shouted.

Jess clapped her hands over her ears to block out the blasting horn as she ran to dial 911. At least her mother's Mercedes hadn't been stolen, but now there was no question about what they'd heard. Someone had tried to get into the car . . . probably the same person who'd made the noise out back! And whoever it was, sure wasn't clowning around.

CHAPTER

2

*H*ONK . . . HONK . . . HONK . . . HONK . . . !

"The police are coming!" Jess shouted over the endless honking, and slammed down her bedroom phone. "I was so hyper I almost forgot our address!"

Outside, a car motor roared up the driveway.

"There's your mom's Jeep!" Cara reported from the front window.

Jess ran to look. Sure enough, Mom was jumping out of the Jeep. Jess unlocked her front door, her palms all sweaty. "Come on, everybody!"

"I'm still stuck in Cara's clown suit!" Becky wailed.

"We'll get you out of it later!" Jess called, running out the door.

As the four of them rushed alongside the new garage addition, Jess held her hands to her ears against the car horn's endless HONK! . . . HONK! . . . HONK! . . . HONK! . . .

Mom raced to the Mercedes in her white pantsuit, key in hand. She poked the key into the driver's door, and the awful honking stopped.

"What's going on?" she demanded, frowning at Jess. Her square chin was firmly set, and she smoothed her long reddish-brown hair farther back off her forehead—a sure sign that she'd had a bad day. "Did you kids fool with my car?"

Jess's heart thumped hard. "Not us! We heard a loud clanging noise out back, then we got some weird phone calls, and then the car alarm went off. We didn't do anything. I just called 911, and the police are on their way."

"The police!" Mom exclaimed. "Sorry, I shouldn't have jumped to conclusions, but I come home to the car alarm honking and you kids in clown suits."

Jess had almost forgotten what they were wearing, and now was no time to worry about it. She explained quickly, since she could already hear a police siren wailing closer and closer.

Mrs. Bay, an elderly neighbor, called from across the street, "What's going on over there?"

"A would-be car thief," Mom answered. "Lock up your house."

Mrs. Bay clapped a hand to her mouth. "I'll warn the neighbors," she called as she shut her door.

Within minutes, a police car pulled up, its siren stopping, but its emergency lights still flashing. Two policemen jumped out. They ran up the driveway, their eyes darting all around, then stopping in surprise when they spotted the four girls dressed as clowns.

"I'm afraid you're too late," Mom said. "Whoever it was is long gone."

The tall, blond policeman introduced himself. "Officer

Drane, ma'am," he said, removing his hat. "And this is Officer Salvio," he said of the shorter, dark-haired man. Officer Drane took a pen and notebook from his pocket. "Can you tell us exactly what happened?"

"I just got here myself," Mom answered. "You can ask my daughter, Jess. She's the clown in red."

Embarrassed, Jess shoved her red yarn bangs back, but they flopped over her eyes again. She scowled. If only this officer weren't pressing his lips together trying not to laugh at her. They probably weren't allowed to laugh while investigating a crime. Finally, she explained the story and he wrote it in his notebook.

"Did you get a look at who was in the vehicle?" he asked.

"We—" Cara stepped forward, suddenly tripping over an ankle ruffle. She grabbed Tricia, almost pulling her down with her. Jess and Tricia let out shrieks of laughter, and Cara and Becky giggled wildly.

"Girls!" Mom warned sternly.

"Did you see who was in the vehicle?" Officer Drane asked again.

Still struggling to untangle her feet from the clown suit, Cara shook her head and tried to look serious. "We couldn't see the street because of those bushes in front of Jess's window."

"How about the vehicle itself?" he asked.

"We only heard it leaving," Jess told him. "It was sputtery, like an old car."

He wrote that down, then gestured toward the girls. "May I ask why you're all wearing clown suits? We . . . ah . . . don't often take reports from . . . uh . . . clowns." His lips quivered from trying not to laugh.

Officer Salvio slapped a hand over his mouth and turned away, his shoulders shaking.

It was a peculiar sight, all right: Cara holding up the huge, blue polka-dot suit and trying to stand up straight, Becky halfway out of Cara's small, yellow outfit, and Tricia, in her green costume, limping along in a one-inch heel dress shoe still on one foot. Jess felt even more stupid in her clown suit and the raggedy red yarn wig flopping over her eyes. If her hair weren't pinned up, she would have pulled the dumb wig off.

She almost giggled, but the policemen might think the whole thing was a joke, so Jess forced herself to be serious. "We're all members of a working club, called the Twelve Candles Club. We were practicing for tomorrow, when we have a job as clowns at a kids' birthday party."

"I see," the officer replied, but his lips still quivered. "Do any of you have something to add to what your friend has told us so far?"

Cara's eyes brightened as she clutched Becky's billowing clown suit away from the dirty driveway. "I just remembered a blue van was parked on the street when we came over. Old and beat-up, like you don't see around here."

"Anyone in it?" Officer Drane asked.

Cara shook her head. "I didn't see anyone."

Becky and Tricia remembered it now, too, but had nothing else to add.

Officer Drane nodded toward the open garage door. "Anything missing in there?"

"I haven't had a chance to look," Mom said. "I left the garage door open this morning. I'm a realtor, and took the Jeep to show some land out in the foothills."

"Better have a look in the garage to see if things are in order," he suggested.

Inside, Jess noticed her bike. "My bike has been moved! I never park it on that side." Then looking up, she exclaimed, "Hey, Dad's pellet gun is missing!"

"A pellet gun?" Officer Drane asked.

Mom nodded. "My husband bought a cheap plastic one last summer to try to get rid of bats under our patio overhang. We heard they sometimes carry rabies."

Jess pointed to a large hook. "The gun always hung there," she told the officer. "Above the badminton rackets."

"Any ammunition in it?" Officer Drane asked.

"No," Mom answered. "We ran out of pellets just about the time the bats flew south. The CO_2 cartridge had given out, too."

The officers continued to look around the almost empty three-car garage. "Anything else missing?"

Mom and Jess glanced around, then shook their heads. The golf clubs and tennis rackets were in place; everything else, like Christmas ornaments, was boxed.

"We'll have to file a report and dust for fingerprints," Officer Drane said. "You're fortunate your car wasn't stolen."

Jess's face turned hot. Leaving a Mercedes parked out front drew attention to them, which Mom liked to do. It was bad enough having a double lot and a custom-built house in Santa Rosita Estates. Almost as embarrassing as standing out front in a clown suit.

"We should set up a Neighborhood Watch," Mom suggested. "I'd be glad to organize it. We could meet here tomorrow night."

Officer Drane took a card from his shirt pocket. "Our Crime Prevention Specialist would be glad to help you set one up, ma'am, but I can't imagine a neighborhood organizing that fast."

"Don't worry, I'll do it," Mom assured him.

The policemen looked skeptical. *They don't know my mother*, Jess thought.

Officer Salvio had gone up the hill by the drainage swale to look for evidence. Returning, he shook his head. "Nothing but an overturned metal watering can on the sidewalk behind the garage. That's probably what made the clanging sound. I also found this gum wrapper." He held up the shred of evidence in a plastic bag. "Anyone in your family chew this brand?"

"I suppose we all have at one time or other," Mom answered. "But none of us go up by the swale. Only the gardener, to trim the ice plant."

Officer Drane took down everyone's name and address, while Officer Salvio dusted Jess's bike and the car door for fingerprints.

Across the street, neighbors gathered to watch. It was unusual to see a police car in the neighborhood, not to mention four clowns.

"Tell me about this Twelve Candles Club," Officer Drane said. "Is that the same girls' club I heard about on TV recently? Seems to me one of you was chased by some dogs to Morelli's Pizza Parlor."

"That's us, all right," Jess said. "Becky Hamilton is our president. She should tell you about it."

"You're the president of this club?" Officer Drane asked.

Becky nodded, her wig flapping around her ears.

Jess clapped a hand to her mouth to keep from laughing, and Becky glared at her.

After she'd explained the club to the officer, he asked, "Do you girls get references from the people you work for?"

"It's one of our rules," Becky answered. "We won't work

for anyone, or take their kids for Morning Fun unless someone we know says they're all right."

"Good," he said. "How many people know that you take phone calls from 4:30 to 5:30?"

"Everyone we work for," she answered, "and everyone who gets our fliers. We're careful about who we give them to, though."

He nodded. "I have some Baby-sitters' Safety Checklist handouts in the car that might be useful for your club. Just a minute, I'll get them."

The girls glanced at one another, pulling their lips together and crossing their eyes, trying not to giggle.

Returning from the car, Officer Drane said, "Baby-sitting is a big responsibility."

"We know," Becky answered, trying to look serious.

"I'm interested in those anonymous phone calls," the officer told Jess. "Let us know if you get more of them."

"Believe me, we will!"

Finally it was over, and the policemen were leaving. Mom jumped into her Mercedes to drive it into the garage. She shook her head, rolling her eyes but half-smiling. "Those poor policemen were dying to laugh, seeing you crazy girls in those crazy clown suits!"

A bubble of laughter escaped Jess as she pointed at Cara. "I don't think I could have stood those officers being here one more minute without cracking up!" She noticed the neighbors across the street still watching, making her laugh harder. "They must think we're a bunch of weirdos!" She gasped, doubling up with giggles. And she wasn't the only one, either.

Cara, Becky, and Tricia were convulsing all around her, laughing like anything.

"I've never felt so wacko as when those officers drove up and saw us in these clown suits!" Tricia gasped. "I suppose they'll tell the whole police force about cross-examining clowns!"

"I was half-expecting a TV van to pull up and film us for the evening news!" Cara laughed. "I wish we would have at least gotten it on video!"

Laughing even harder, Jess held her stomach and ran for her room. Once inside, she flung herself to the floor, followed by her three friends. They'd made it! They rolled on the carpet, laughing hysterically, as if it were a wild celebration. They'd made it through the whole crazy ordeal!

———

By dinnertime, matters no longer seemed so funny. A burglar had been lurking around her house! Jess felt shaky as she stood at the family room table and dished salad from the huge wooden salad bowl into a small one.

All three of her brothers sat watching her.

"You scared, Jess?" asked Garner, her eighteen-year-old brother. Santa Rosita High's star quarterback was tall, square-chinned, red-haired, and handsome.

She shot an irked look at him across the round table. "Who me? No way."

He shrugged. "You look like it to me, kiddo."

"Kiddo, yourself!" she snapped. "Even if I were scared, Dad wouldn't like you teasing me about it."

"You're crazy!" Garner answered, then leaned back in his chair and laughed at her.

Jess stuck her tongue out at him. At least Mom had promised not to tell them about her and the rest of the club being in clown suits when the police questioned them.

Serving the salads, she looked at her brothers. They'd had a swim in the pool when they'd come home, and their red hair was still damp. As they helped themselves to spaghetti, they discussed the robbery—and looked a little too innocent, especially Jordan.

Whoa! she thought, suspicious.

"I know it's a dumb question," she began, "but it wouldn't be the first time you've tried to scare me. Did you guys make some noise out back this afternoon? . . . or set off the car alarm?"

As usual, Garner took charge, his blue eyes meeting hers. "Mom already grilled us, and *none* of us were even here. *None* of us. You know we were all at work."

He and their seventeen-year-old brother, Jordan, were working this summer at The Household Place, driving forklifts and muscling around boxes and crates. It was a good job for football players like them, so they could stay in shape.

Jess glanced at Jordan, who had the curliest and brightest red hair. One thing she usually liked about him was his mischievous streak, but right now he was busy slopping mayo on his spaghetti. He'd slather the whole mess between slices of garlic bread, as usual. "How about you, Jordan? Did you do it?"

"Come *on*, Jess!" he protested. "Garn already said we were at work. Besides, you know we wouldn't be peering in the window. Do you think we're weird or something? As for the Mercedes, we have enough cars without wanting to tool around in that big boat."

She turned to Mark. He was blue-eyed like the others, but had lots of freckles and didn't care two cents for sports. "You, Mark?"

"You think I'm crazy enough to do something that'd make me lose my driver's license?" he asked.

"I guess not," she answered, remembering how badly he'd wanted it. "Just thought I should ask."

"Besides, why would any of us steal that stupid pellet gun?" Garner asked. "It doesn't even shoot straight. You know how Dad had to point it way off to shoot those bats."

Jess pounced. "How'd you know the pellet gun was stolen?"

Mark laughed. "Because Mom told us, that's how!"

"Oh," Jess answered, grinning sheepishly as they laughed. Nonetheless, she still felt a little suspicious about them. "I wish we still had Ace," she said about their old German shepherd, who'd died two years ago. No sense in wishing about him or any other dog, though. Mom said pets were just trouble.

"How do you know it was only one burglar?" Mark asked.

Jess shrugged. "I don't know. Maybe it just seems better to think there's only one."

Mom brought a basket of garlic bread to the table and sat down between Garner and Mark. "Wait until your father hears about it. I suppose he'll want to put in a house alarm system, and the blasted thing will always be going off at the wrong times, with you kids rushing in and out the doors."

Jess took the last salad and sat down herself.

No one spoke for a while, then Mom said, "After this afternoon's trouble, we're going to have to be careful to lock the doors and windows. Whoever was here might come again."

"Let's not talk about it anymore," Jess pleaded.

Then everyone was eating, and she wished for an instant that they said grace before meals, like in Tricia's and Becky's families.

The next morning was Tuesday, and after stopping across the street for Cara, Jess and she rode their bikes up La Crescenta Drive to pick up Tricia and Becky, ten houses away. They'd cleaned house for Mrs. O'Lone last week and knew it'd take exactly twenty minutes to ride to her oceanside house.

"Were you scared last night?" Cara asked as they rode along. "Your room is so far off, by itself—"

"I was for a while," Jess admitted, pedaling along. "Then I'd just think of being in our clown outfits when the police came, and it made things more funny." In truth, she'd been terrified, hearing noises outside her window half the night.

"I thought maybe you'd sleep up in the guest room," Cara said.

"I'd never hear the end of it from my brothers if I did," Jess answered. "Anyhow, Mom came to my room for a while, and we went through my closet to see what I'd outgrown. It wasn't much." She put on a burst of speed, not wanting to think about the trouble. She turned her attention to the red geraniums and bougainvillea that bloomed all over the neighborhood.

"Hey, Jess!" Cara yelled. "Aren't we stopping for Tricia and Becky?"

Jess slammed on her bike's brakes. She'd already ridden past Becky's. "Whoa! My brain was a thousand miles away!" She made a U-turn and pedaled back.

Cara straddled her bike in Tricia's driveway. "You positive you're not scared? I sure was last night in my room. I could hardly sleep. I figured whoever it was might try my house next. You know, he could be one of those robbers who concentrates on one neighborhood."

"On the TV news, they said the burglaries are in the richer neighborhoods," Jess said.

When Tricia and Becky rode their bikes out, they were joking about yesterday's clown episode. Then Cara and Jess started on burglar stories like the one about a burglar who always hit the same types of houses in a development.

Tricia moaned. "Probably just two-story houses!"

The Bennetts lived in a two-story development model, though, not a two-story custom house like Jess's.

"Come on!" Jess said, putting on another burst of speed. "We'll be late! And working for Mrs. O'Lone every Tuesday this summer is too good a job to lose."

Pretty soon they crossed Ocean Avenue and turned left, riding downhill in the bike lane. As they passed Morelli's, Jess remembered her surprise. "Hey, Mom says we can have a slumber party at my house Sunday night . . . Morelli's pizza, of course!"

"Hey, all right!" Becky yelled behind her. "You want me to pass it on?"

"Sure. Better ask if Cara and Tricia will be back from L.A. in time."

Despite the sounds of traffic, Jess heard them pass the slumber party invitation back. Before long, Becky yelled, "All right! They'll be back in time! We think we can all come! We just have to get permission!"

Jess blew out her breath in relief. They'd have a wacko time like they used to and, by then, they'd probably have forgotten all about the burglar. In a few minutes, they'd clean for Mrs. O'Lone, and life would be back to normal.

The O'Lones lived in an old two-story Spanish house. It was harder to clean than the newer, modern houses in Santa

Rosita Estates, but Mrs. O'Lone liked to have all four of them working together—one of the reasons for having the club.

Jess liked hearing the muffled roar of the ocean as they parked their bikes around behind the O'Lone's garage. Today, she felt like doing something really physical. "I'll vacuum and wash floors," she offered.

Mrs. O'Lone shuffled out the back door to greet them. She was a frail, graying woman. "Good morning, girls," she said. "What's new?"

"We were robbed yesterday," Jess blurted.

"You, too?" Mrs. O'Lone asked. "Why, someone has tried to break into nearly every house on this block. I was just going to tell you to put your bikes in the garage."

"Not here, too!" Jess said.

They trooped back to their bikes. "And I was hoping to forget all about it," Jess groaned.

"You're the one who mentioned it to her," Cara told her.

Jess nodded. "Guess I was asking for it."

When their bikes were locked in the garage, they headed for the house again.

"Yikes!" Cara yelled. "Look! It's that old blue van going by out there! I'm sure of it! The one we saw parked in front of Jess's house yesterday!"

They raced out to the street, but the battered van was turning the corner and disappeared. No chance to get a license number or even to see how many people were in it.

Jess drew a discouraged breath. "We'd better call the police and tell them anyhow. I'm sure they all know who we are. I can already hear them saying, 'You know, that goofy girls' club, the ones in the crazy clown suits.' "

CHAPTER

3

When Jess coasted her bike into the driveway the next afternoon, she was glad to see her father's old leave-at-the-airport white Toyota parked in its usual spot behind the garage. Everything would be fine, now that Dad was home. She parked her bike next to his car, hoping he wasn't sleeping. After flights to Taiwan, Singapore, and Hong Kong, he sometimes went straight to bed.

Excited, she unlocked her front door and raced through her bedroom. The red light on her answering machine blinked steadily, but she ignored it.

"Dad?" she yelled, letting herself through the inside door to the main part of the house.

"Out here on the patio!"

She felt like doing a handspring right there, but instead, ran through the family room and out the sliding screen door.

He sat at the glass-topped table near the pool. "There's my

girl!" His smile was like sunshine to Jess, and he stood up, opening his arms wide.

She rushed to him, glad to be in his arms. Jess could smell the familiar scent of his spicy after-shave lotion. Somehow, being held by Dad made the blue-van man seem very far away.

"Hey, you little powerhouse, you're going to squeeze me to death," he teased. "Not that I mind being squeezed by my daughter."

She laughed, then stood back to look at him. She had a handsome Dad—slim, tall, with a nice tan, and brown hair with only a hint of gray. He looked especially good in his white tennis outfit. "It's great to have you home, Dad," Jess said.

"It's great to be home, believe me. How was gymnastics practice yesterday?"

"Good . . . really good."

He pulled out a chair for her and patted the cushion. "Sit down and tell me all about the trouble while I eat yesterday's leftover spaghetti."

Jess sat down, hating to talk about it. "What trouble?" she asked.

His eyes, hazel like hers, were serious. "The burglar, Jess. Mom mentioned it on the phone a few minutes ago."

Jess flopped back against the chair cushion. "The latest is that Cara saw the burglar's old blue van this morning. She spotted it when we were cleaning at Mrs. O'Lone's house, so we called the police."

"What did they say?"

"That they'd send a detective to check on it. By the time I explained the location to two different people, the van was probably a thousand miles away."

"Mom says she's setting up a Neighborhood Watch," Dad

said. "In the meantime, we'll have to be more careful."

Jess nodded glumly. "I guess so."

"No guessing about it. Did you leave your bike out?"

Jess almost jumped from her chair. "I forgot! I was so excited to see your car . . . Oh! and we've got a party-helper job at two o'clock. I've got to eat and run."

"Come on," he said, "I'll give you a hand with your bike. Then you can heat up some spaghetti for yourself."

As they passed through the family room, he grabbed the garage door opener and frowned. Jess saw his expression and muttered, "It's not fair that someone could give our family such a scare, is it?"

"My thoughts exactly," her father replied.

They went out the front door, and once past the acacia bushes, Dad scanned the driveway. "The coast is clear," he announced. "No spooks now."

Jess smiled a little, then headed for her bike as her father zapped open the garage door. "Maybe you'd better check the garage to see if anything else is missing," Jess called over her shoulder. "Mom and I were pretty rattled when the police were here."

He followed her into the garage, looking around as she parked her bike. "Nope, just that cheap pellet gun. Poor guy doesn't have much judgment, stealing such a junker."

"I guess not," Jess said, feeling the same nervous flutters she'd felt yesterday. "Are you going to play tennis now?" she asked, eyeing his outfit.

"Not if you want me to stay home, Jess."

"I guess I do, until I leave anyhow," she said. "All of a sudden, I don't feel right being alone yet. But I don't want you to cancel your game just because—"

Her father pressed a finger to her lips. "I don't want you feeling *wrong* alone."

She smiled. "Are you sure?" Usually he wouldn't cancel a tennis game for anything.

"I'm sure." He led the way from the garage.

Out in the sunshine, Jess glanced down the street. No blue van down there now—at least none that she could see. Maybe the burglar, whoever he was, wouldn't come back.

"Come on, get some lunch. You're safe with your old dad."

"I know. I just wish you weren't gone so often."

"Me, too. Say, I hear you girls are doing some clowning at a birthday party. That should be fun."

"Yeh. I just hope we can pull it off," Jess said. The rest of the club had practiced yesterday while she was at gymnastics. "I sure do hope so."

———

Just after one o'clock, Jess arrived at Tricia's, a peach two-story house that looked as warm and welcoming now as when they had their Monday, Wednesday, and Friday sessions of Morning Fun for Kids. She was relieved to hear her friends in the backyard laughing. "I'm here!" Jess yelled over the side gate.

"Bring your bike in!" Tricia yelled from around back.

"Whoops . . . I'm always forgetting!"

She dragged her bike in through the side gate and breezeway. "Whoa!" she exclaimed when she saw them all dressed in their clown costumes.

"Ta-da!" Tricia said dramatically, throwing out an arm for emphasis. "The Polka-Dot Clowns!"

"Sounds good," Jess answered, impressed at how great they looked. "You know, you all look like r-e-a-l clowns!"

Tricia bowed in her billowy green suit, then bobbed up. "I'm Jingles, and I say, you're on for makeup, Jess McColl." Tricia's own makeup was perfect: a big red smiley mouth, red circles on her cheeks, a red foam-rubber nose, thick dark eyebrows, and green triangles above and below her green eyes. She did a comical tap dance, making the bells on her wrists and ankles jingle.

Jess glanced at Cara—or rather Lello—all in yellow, except for her bright make-up. Beck-o the Clown looked just as good in her blue baggy outfit. "I can't believe it's you guys!" Jess exclaimed, excited now to get her own outfit on.

Lello and Beck-o both bowed. "I really *feel* like a clown," Becky-Beck-o said. "I didn't think I could do the skits, but being all done up like a clown should help."

Cara-Lello nodded her moppy yellow head. "Sure makes me feel different."

"I'm glad you all have smiley faces," Jess said.

They grinned, making their big red lips turn up even more.

"Mrs. Bennett says it's best for little kids," Becky-Beck-o explained. "Smiley faces won't scare them like a frown might."

"Makes sense," Jess said.

"Excuse'a, please," Tricia-Jingles announced. "We have to practice our routines."

"Excuse'a, me!" Jess laughed, parking her bike on the patio. Grabbing the bag with her clown suit and wig, she hurried to the redwood patio table, where Tricia's mother waited with a makeup kit.

"I hear your new name is Fireplug," Mrs. Bennett said with a friendly smile.

Jess nodded. "It fits my shape."

Mrs. Bennett laughed. "And your personality. Now, hop

into your clown suit, then have a seat on this bench."

Mrs. Bennett not only knew about costumes, but makeup, too. She volunteered at the Christian Youth Theater, where Tricia sometimes acted. Becky and Tricia had attended a clowning class there. Sometimes Jess wished she could be part of it, but she was too busy with gymnastics. *Besides*, Jess thought, *Mom doesn't care much for that Christian stuff.*

Jess pulled on her clown suit over her shorts and shirt. "I'm glad I only have to do tumbling."

Tricia's mother's blue eyes sparkled. "I'm certain you'd be good at any of it."

"How's come?" Jess asked, plopping down on the bench.

Mrs. Bennett wrapped an old sheet around Jess's shoulders. "Because there's nothing at all wishy-washy about you, Jessica McColl. You're a girl of action. I fully expect to see you in the Olympics someday. When you go after something, it's as good as done."

Jess didn't know what to say, but smiled while Mrs. Bennett pinned up her hair. After that, she smeared cold, white goop all over her face. Next came powder, big brown eyebrows, red cheeks and mouth, and green triangles above and below her eyes. Finally, Mrs. Bennett stuck on the red foam-rubber nose. "Oooh, this thing itches," Jess yelped, wiggling her nose.

Mrs. Bennett laughed, then sat back to study her work. "Well, not bad, if I do say so myself. Now, let me put that red wig on you. I'll use lots of long hairpins, but you'll have to be sure the elastic in back is snug so the wig doesn't fly off while you're tumbling."

Jess giggled, imagining it.

After the wig was in place, Mrs. Bennett turned the

makeup case around so Jess could look in the mirror inside the lid. "Introducing Fireplug!"

Jess stared in the mirror. "I can't believe it's me! It really looks good! Thanks, Mrs. Bennett."

"My pleasure. Looking the part is one of the most important aspects of acting. You not only fool the audience, but you can fool yourself."

"I hope it works today!" Jess said.

"Here's the party agenda," Mrs. Bennett said.

Jess read the list.

1. Face-painting as kids arrive
2. Hokey-Pokey
3. Sing "Old MacDonald Had a Farm"
4. Comedy Show (balloon skit, elastic skit, vegetable-stand skit)
5. Balloon animals
6. Birthday present circle
7. Clown gifts for kids

"Time to go!" Becky-Beck-o yelled, heading for her bike. "You look perfect, Fireplug!"

"Yeh, perfectly funny!" Jess laughed, flopping her baggy outfit out by the pockets. But she knew if Becky, the artist among them, said she looked perfect, then she did. Jess followed behind them to their bikes. "Who's driving us?"

Tricia-Jingles blinked at her. "We're riding our bikes. Mom has to stay here because Suzanne and Bryan are taking naps."

"You're kidding!" Jess said, her mouth dropping open. "We're going to ride our bikes through the streets in these clown suits?"

"It's only six blocks to Davis's," Tricia-Jingles said. "Besides, no one will know who we are."

"I guess not," Jess decided.

"We'll ride as fast as the wind," Tricia-Jingles assured her, and began to quote dramatically, "Wind is to show . . . how a thing can blow . . . and especially through trees—"

"Never mind!" Jess laughed. "Let's go!"

Mrs. Bennett held the side gate open for them. "You'd better pull the pant legs of your costumes up over your knees so they don't get greasy from your bike chains."

Jess tugged at the elastic on both legs, then climbed onto her bike. "We look weirder than ever now, with these outfits billowing above our knees!"

"I think you all look great," Mrs. Bennett insisted. "You'll be a treat for Santa Rosita! Do you have the bag with supplies, Tricia? And the face-painting kit?"

"On my bike."

Mrs. Bennett smiled at them. "I'll pray for all of you that everything goes well."

"We'll need it, Mom," Tricia-Jingles said, waving as she rode out onto the street.

Jess rode down the driveway last, behind Cara-Lello. "I sure hope my brothers don't see me!"

"Or my sister and her snooty friends," Cara-Lello added as they pedaled onto the street.

Jess peered about. No neighbors so far.

The street was quiet for a warm June afternoon. At the first corner, though, four or five drivers in cars stared, and two wide-eyed kids pointed their fingers and yelled, "Clowns!"

"Wait till we get to Ocean Avenue!" Jess predicted.

"Don't worry, Tricia's got it figured out," Cara-Lello assured her. "We hang back until the traffic light turns green, then we race across."

"Good idea," Jess said, still nervous. "I know it seems impossible, especially with this red nose right in the middle of my face, but I can't help thinking someone might know who we are."

"No way!" Cara-Lello answered, sounding confident.

As they neared Ocean Avenue in the bike lane, Tricia-Jingles and Becky-Beck-o slowed down. "Remember, when the light turns green, we ride like anything!" Tricia-Jingles called back.

But as they approached the intersection, the traffic light turned red, and cars began to line up just as the four clowns rode up.

"Oh no!" Jess groaned over her shoulder at Cara as one driver after another turned to stare.

"You know it," Cara-Lello said in dismay.

"Hey, you!" a high school guy yelled. "Where's the circus?" His friends in the car with him all burst out laughing.

Tricia-Jingles cackled in her best old-lady voice, "Why, hello there, son-ny boy! Ain't you the sweet-est thing?"

He shrunk back into his seat, as embarrassed as Jess felt. At least *she* had a disguise on!

Finally the light turned green, and the four clowns pedaled furiously up to Ocean Avenue, then screeched to a stop. "Yipes!" Jess yelped, almost rear-ending Becky-Beck-o. An elderly couple hadn't made it all the way through the crosswalk.

Now she and the others sat on their bikes—in full view of Ocean Avenue! It seemed as if every car in the world began to honk at them. Jess felt her face grow warmer and warmer, and thought her makeup might melt and run off.

"I've never been so embarrassed!" Jess groaned. She could hardly hear her own voice over the din, and all she could see were the laughing faces of what seemed like half the population of Santa Rosita.

As if it weren't bad enough, Tricia-Jingles wagged her hand at the honking drivers. "How-deee, folks!" she croaked in her old-lady voice, "How-deee!"

Drivers called out to them, laughing, and it seemed forever before the old couple stepped up from the bike lane and onto the curb.

"Ride!" Jess shouted. "Ride like anything!"

Cars honked, and truck horns blared. Halfway across the intersection, the racket almost split Jess's eardrums. She even spotted Officers Drane and Salvio in their police car, laughing along with everyone else. Jess pedaled harder, her clown suit billowing out behind her. Finally, they left Ocean Avenue and the horrendous honking behind them.

"We'll have to cross again on the way home," Jess complained, "and traffic will be worse then."

"No one knew who we were!" Cara-Lello insisted.

"Except Officers Drane and Salvio. They knew who we were all right." Jess was silent for a moment, then burst out laughing as the whole wacko scene hit her full force.

Tricia-Jingles, Cara-Lello, and Becky-Beck-o all glanced back at her, then started to giggle, too.

The four of them pedaled hard for the two remaining blocks, then turned up the driveway to the Davis house. "We made it!" Tricia-Jingles yelled. "See, the garage door is even open. We park inside, then pop out the side door into their backyard."

Jess coasted alongside Cara-Lello. "Now all we have to do is pull off this clown party for those wild Davis twins," she muttered.

"Tricia's got it all figured out," Cara-Lello said.

Jess drew a deep breath. "Let's hope it's nothing like her figuring out how to cross Ocean Avenue unnoticed!"

They parked their bikes in the Davis garage and adjusted their pant legs and ruffles. "Ready?" Tricia-Jingles asked.

Jess checked the elastic on her wig. "Ready as we'll ever be."

Tricia waved her hand like a baton, and they popped out the side door of the garage and into the backyard, singing loudly, "Happy birthday to you. . . !"

Jojo and Jimjim grabbed their mother's hands. Their green eyes widened and even the freckles on their noses seemed to pale.

"Happy birthday, dear Jojo and Jimjim," the girls chorused. "Happy birthday to you!"

Becky, having baby-sat for them, knew them best. "Wow!" she exclaimed, "you're five years old!"

Jojo and Jimjim hid behind their mother's skirt.

"They're scared!" Tricia whispered.

Whoa, what if they start crying? Jess thought. All of their work and plans for more clown parties would be ruined. Suddenly she knew what to do. "Watch Fireplug the Clown," she called, flinging herself over into a backflip. Luckily, her wig elastic stayed snug.

The boys edged out from behind their mother to watch, and Jess cartwheeled all around the lawn.

"Umpty-dumpty-dum-dum-a-lum!" they yelled, using their secret twin language. They flung themselves over, trying to turn cartwheels, too.

"Not just yet, boys," Mrs. Davis said. "You'll get your nice green playsuits dirty before your guests arrive. And I do believe I hear a car now—yes, it's your guests coming!"

Soon two girls and a boy stepped into the backyard. Tricia-

Jingles did a dance for them, the bells on her wrists and ankles jingling away. "I'm Jingles. May I take your birthday gifts for Jojo and Jimjim to the birthday table?"

The kids gave up their presents without a word, awed at the sight of four clowns. Jess turned more flips, hoping she'd last through the whole two-hour party. This could be more exhausting than the Olympics.

Luckily, Tricia gave her a break by asking, "May we clowns paint your faces? We can paint hearts, rainbows, spiders, and shooting stars."

"Hearts!" a girl piped. "I want hearts!"

"Spiders!" the boy said. "Big scary spiders!"

Jojo and Jimjim yelled together, " 'Tooting 'tars!"

As more kids arrived, Jess felt like the party just might be a success. Mrs. Davis talked to parents and answered phone calls while Cara-Lello greeted the children and took their gifts to the birthday table. Jess did a few more handsprings, and Becky-Beck-o and Tricia-Jingles painted the new arrival's faces. Finally, all twelve of Jimjim's and Jojo's guests had arrived—and the noise level was getting louder and l-o-u-d-e-r.

Tricia-Jingles stood up and jingled her wrist bells over their heads. "And now, if everyone will form a circle, the Polka-dot Clowns will lead you in dancing the world-famous *Hokey-Pokey*."

Jess grabbed the hands of two kids, who stared uneasily at her. "Jingles will show us how to do the Hokey-Pokey," she said encouragingly.

"All right! Let's do it!" Tricia-Jingles said. "You put your right foot in, you put your right foot out. . . ."

Next, they all sat cross-legged on the patio for a rousing version of "Old MacDonald Had a Farm."

When they'd finished the song, Jingles told them, "While you're all still sitting down, I want to ask you a v-e-r-y-i-m-p-o-r-t-a-n-t question." She pulled a long blue balloon from the pocket of her baggy green outfit. "I . . . ah . . . don't know what this is, do you?"

"A balloon!" one of the kids yelled.

"It's a *bal-loon!*" the others chorused.

Getting into her character, Tricia-Jingles inspected it closely. "Oh, I thought balloons were supposed to be round." She looked puzzled. "What am I supposed to do with a balloon?"

"Blow it up!" the kids yelled.

"How?" Jingles asked. "How do you blow it up?"

Some of the kids giggled.

One shouted, "Put it in your mouth and blow."

Tricia-Jingles wadded up the balloon, stuffed the whole thing in her mouth, and blew it out. "Like that?"

"No! No!" they yelled, more of them laughing. "Just blow in the hole!"

Tricia-Jingles put the balloon's hole to her mouth and blew hard. Then she inhaled the air again, her cheeks puffing out and her eyes bugging out.

"*NO!*" they shouted. "YOU LEAVE THE AIR INSIDE THE BALLOON!"

"Ohhh, I get it!" Jingles answered with a big grin, finally filling the balloon with air.

"Now what do I do with it?" Jingles asked.

"TIE IT UP!" the kids shouted between laughing. "SO THE AIR WON'T GO OUT!"

Jingles tied it to her finger. "Like this?"

"NO!" they yelled, laughing harder and harder. "NO, YOU LET IT GO!"

Jingles blinked hard at them. "Well, if you say so. Here goes!" With that, she let it sail away through the air.

The kids laughed hysterically. When they'd calmed down, Cara-Lello brought Tricia-Jingles a long white piece of elastic with a red pompom tied to each end.

"Look," Jingles said. "I have a new invention. Lello, you hold that end, and I'll hold this end. Now, let's stretch this thing as far as it will go." When the elastic was stretched to its limit, Jingles added, "Now, I'll say, 'Ring, ring, ring—I have a phone call for you.' Then you say, 'Let me have it.' "

Lello looked at her red pompom from every angle, then nodded happily.

Jingles yelled, "Ring, ring, ring!" Putting her pompom to her ear, she said, "I have a phone call for you!"

Lello smiled, looking simple. "I wonder if it's my Aunt Suzie from Minneapolis?"

"No, no, no!" Jingles answered. "When I say, 'I have a phone call for you,' you say, 'Let me have it.' Now, let's try it again."

Lello nodded.

Jingles grinned mischievously at the kids, then turned to Lello. "Ring, ring, ring!" She put the red pompom to her ear again. "I have a phone call for you."

Lello jumped excitedly. "I wonder if it's my friend, calling to ask me to a ball game!"

"NO, NO, NO!" Jingles yelled impatiently. "When I say, 'I have a phone call for you,' you say, 'Let me have it.' Ready?"

Lello shrugged, then said, "Ready."

"Ring, ring—"

"WAIT!" Lello interrupted. "What do I say?"

"*Let me have it!*" Jingles bellowed.

Lello let go of the elastic band, knocking Jingles down with the pompom, while the kids roared with laughter.

Next was a crazy skit called "The Vegetable Stand." Jingles chased after Beck-o and Lello, pounding them with a sponge hammer. When Jingles ran after Fireplug, she did handsprings to escape, and the kids laughed even harder.

After that, Jingles and Beck-o made balloon animals for the kids, and Lello and Fireplug handed them out while the kids ate birthday cake and ice cream.

When it was time to give Jojo and Jimjim their birthday gifts, Fireplug, Lello, and Beck-o seated the kids in a circle, and Jingles brought out a plastic bottle with bells tied to it. "I'll spin the bottle. Whoever the bottle points to gives their present to Jojo and Jimjim."

The kids bounced and squealed with excitement.

Once the gift-giving game was underway, Jess helped Becky-Beck-o bring their own presents for the kids from the garage.

Becky had drawn a picture-to-color of four clowns playing tricks on one another, then photocopied them. On the bottom, she'd lettered:

THE POLKA-DOT CLOWNS:
Birthday Parties, Picnics,
and Programs of all kinds.

Below that, she'd printed Jess's phone number. When the mothers came for their kids around four o'clock, Becky gave out the fliers to them. Everyone looked as pleased with the clowns as Mrs. Davis. Several said they'd call them to help at their kids' birthday parties.

When everyone had gone, Mrs. Davis paid the girls and

said, "I couldn't have had such a wonderful party for my boys without you."

"Thanks," Jess said. "We had a lot of fun ourselves."

"All right!" Tricia yelled as they headed for their bikes. "We did it! Yeah for the Crazy Clown Caper!"

"Caper? What's that?" Jess asked.

"A wild performance, an adventure . . . something wild."

"Then it was a caper all right," Jess agreed, climbing onto her bike.

"I thought we did all right," Cara said, hiking up her pant legs as they rode out the driveway. "I wish we had it on video. We could show it to advertise for more jobs."

Jess grinned. "You know, I don't even care if every car on Ocean Avenue honks at us. The Polka-dot Clowns have arrived!"

They rode down the street, not caring about traffic lights holding them up or car horns honking. When they arrived at the corner, though, the horns were louder than ever.

When the light turned green at Ocean Avenue, they set off in unison.

Jess waved dramatically at the drivers as she pedaled across the wide avenue. She felt like a clown in a circus parade. "Have a *great* day!" she called out. Before, on the way to the party, she'd worried about how she looked, but now she didn't care. It was fun to make people laugh. Besides, seeing wacko clowns riding bikes would give the drivers something funny to tell their families.

She yelled again, "Have a g-r-e-a-t day!"

Her words were still ringing out across the traffic when she saw it in the distance—the battered blue van!

CHAPTER

4

There he is!" Jess yelled into the blare of honking horns as she pedaled her bike across Ocean Avenue. "There, in the blue van!" Where were Officers Drane and Salvio now that she needed them? Despite all of the traffic, not a single police car was in sight. If she weren't dressed like a clown, maybe someone would see she was on to something important.

"He's there!" Jess yelled again, pointing at the van. Not even her fellow clowns heard as they biked on ahead through the awful din. Instead, they were waving grandly at the cars, just as she had done moments ago.

Desperate, she shouted, "Don't any of you see it?"

Not one of her friends turned their shaggy clown heads.

Nearly across Ocean Avenue, Jess kept her eyes on the blue van. It was about half a block away and maneuvering into the slow lane. Now it turned off into an old, shabby shopping center. *He saw me pointing!* She knew it. And he'd probably seen her in the clown suit through her window yesterday, too. He knew who she was!

Finally, Jess was in the bike lane of their street, La Crescenta, right behind her friends. The blare of the horns had faded into the background. "Didn't you guys see that blue van?" she shouted as she caught up with them. "I yelled like everything!"

The three slowed their bikes, their smiley clown mouths dropping open. "Are you sure it was the same van?" Tricia asked.

Jess braked to a stop, and the others followed suit. "I'm sure! He turned into that beat-up shopping center where they sell brakes and mufflers and stuff—you know, auto parts."

"Let's call the police," Cara said, a frown creasing the white paint on her face.

"We'd better be sure he's still there first," Becky suggested. "He could have just pulled in there for a minute."

"I think he saw me pointing at him," Jess said.

"Whoa!" Tricia exclaimed. "He *saw* you?"

Jess nodded. "It was a dumb thing to do, I know, but I was trying to get *someone* to notice." She thought for a second. "Maybe we should ride back there. You know, just ride by the shopping center to see if he's still around."

"And have those horns honking at us again?" Cara asked. "Twice was enough for me. Besides, what if he's dangerous."

"Definitely dangerous," Becky said. "And it's almost time for our meeting. I think we should just call the police, tell them we spotted the van, and not get involved. No one will take four clowns seriously. It was hard enough yesterday when the police came to your house, even with your mother there."

Jess felt deflated. "I guess so. Let's just go home."

"I'll call the police from my house," Tricia promised. "Anyhow, Mom has to take off our makeup. You can be first, Jess, so you can get home in time for phone calls."

A passing car honked, then another, as Jess pulled ahead of the others on her bike, leading the way.

Tricia called the police as soon as they reached her house while her mother removed Jess's clown makeup. When Tricia hung up the phone, she said, "They're going to get a detective on it right away."

"Let's hope this is the end of that creep," Jess said. "It was bad enough to find out he was over by the ocean-side houses, but now he's near our neighborhood again."

Five minutes later Jess was on her way home, her clown outfit in a bag on her bike rack. When she approached her driveway she noticed Dad's white Toyota was missing, and she guessed he was out playing tennis. In fact, the garage was empty, so she knew she was home alone.

She locked her bike in the garage, then unlocked her bedroom door and peered in. She'd left the mini-blinds closed, and coming in from the bright sunlight, her room seemed d-a-r-k. She flipped on the overhead lights.

"Fireplug, in the closet you go," she spoke to her clown suit, just to break the silence. She quickly jerked open her closet door. *No one in here.*

She peeked out a slat of the front mini-blinds before opening them. Much better. Sunlight streaming in helped a lot. Then she went to the back blinds and lifted a slat. Just the usual bees hovering over the purple ice plant. *I guess I'll leave this one shut.*

Jess went to her desk. The red light on her answering machine blinked three times, stopped, then blinked three times again. She set the machine to *messages*. The machine rolled back the tape, then began to hum. There was no voice, only a long, crackly hum that made the hair on the back of her neck prickle.

Finally, the caller hung up.

The second call was from Mrs. Davis, thanking the club again for a good job at the party, and letting them know that a cousin of her boys would be attending Morning Fun for Kids tomorrow because he'd had such a good time at the party.

The third call was another horrible hum-m-m-m.

Jess caught a glimmer of movement at the front window. Something was definitely moving!

She picked up the phone, a finger poised at the nine, her eyes glued to the front.

Phew! Jess let out a long sigh of relief. A bird flew up from the bush at her window.

"Phooey!" she spoke loudly to no one but herself. "Phooey on being scared!"

She plopped down on her blue gym mat and began her warm-ups. First head rotations, then body rolls and half arches. She hadn't had time to work on her vaulting today, but she had to keep her body conditioned. She'd work until she was so strong that no one could ever scare her again. She was up to torso circles when the phone rang.

Drawing a deep breath, she stood, walked slowly to the telephone. "Hello. Twelve Candles Club."

No one answered. There was only the awful, ominous hum-m-m-m.

"Hello? *Hel-lo?*"

"Grrrmmmppphhh!" someone growled.

Jess clenched her fists and yelled into the phone. "Listen,

whoever you are, the police are on to you—you stupid creep!"

She suddenly felt weak all over, which made her even more angry at the creep on the phone. A gymnast needed strength—not wobbly knees.

A sharp knock at her front door made her jump, and Jess asked in a quavery voice, "Who . . . who's there?"

"It's us," Cara answered. "Who'd you think?"

"Coming!"

Jess hurried across the room, then peeked out the window before opening the door. Cara, Becky, and Tricia, looking completely normal in their shorts and T-shirts, stood waiting with puzzled looks on their faces.

"Whew, am I glad to see you!" Jess said, letting them in.

"What's wrong *now*?" Tricia asked.

"Just some phone calls with no voice, and then someone growled at me like a prehistoric monster," Jess told them. "Get in here so I can lock the door."

As soon as they were inside, she flipped the dead bolt. Cara, Tricia, and Becky were staring at the back mini-blind, as uptight as she felt.

"It's not right for one guy to give our whole neighborhood the creeps," Cara complained. "It's just not right."

"That's exactly what I told my dad today," Jess told them.

Tricia sighed. "Gramp says that's what evil does. It messes up everything and everyone around it. 'Course, the same thing's true of good—the influence I mean, only it blesses. You know, the opposite of evil."

"*Evil?*" Jess repeated. "What makes you think this person is really and truly evil?"

"Well, people don't talk much about it, but Gramp says there are two spiritual forces in the universe. One is good, and one is evil. Sooner or later everyone decides to follow one or the other. They decide to worship and obey God, or follow the evil side and please themselves. This guy has decided against God and for himself by stealing."

"Something else, too," Becky said. "He's not treating people like he'd want them to treat him—you know, this bad-o probably wouldn't like to be scared or robbed himself."

"Guess I hadn't thought of it like that," Jess admitted. She walked over to the twin beds and sat down. "And, you know what? I don't want to think about it, either! Let's talk about something else."

"We can't," Cara argued. "We've got to deal with it. Already my father thinks I should drop out of TCC until the police find the burglar. I'm afraid to even mention anything about the phantom phone calls or your seeing the blue van again, let alone your slumber party Sunday night."

"You're kidding!" Jess said.

Cara shook her head. "I'm not, Jess. I wish I were."

Becky nodded. "My mom says we'll have to wait and see if things have calmed down by then. Maybe the police will have caught whoever it was."

"My mom said about the same thing," Tricia added.

"Ufffff!" Jess groaned. "I'd like to pound that no-good burglar until he's too scared to bother anyone again!"

Tricia grinned a little. "If he saw you this mad, he'd probably run for his life! But you know what, Jess? Gramp says we have to forgive our enemies, even criminals."

"Forgive them? No *way*!" Jess objected. "Come on, let's start the meeting."

Becky pulled out the desk chair and sat down. "This meeting of the Twelve Candles Club shall now come to order," she announced. "Cara, will you read the minutes of the last meeting?"

Jess only half-listened as Cara read the minutes and Tricia gave the treasurer's report. Her eyes kept wandering to the front window. Maybe tonight she'd sleep in the guest bedroom, even if her brothers teased her.

"We need to pay another three dollars each for Morning Fun for Kids snacks and craft materials," Tricia was saying. "And some of you still haven't paid for the clown outfits. I had to use my own money to pay my mother for the stuff."

Jess got up to get her wallet on top of her desk. *It's not here!* Her heart almost stopped, then she remembered she'd hidden it under some T-shirts in her chest of drawers. She crossed the room and opened the drawer. It was a relief to feel the wallet in her hands—not that it held so much money, but she'd worked plenty hard for what was there.

Tricia checked their names off as they each paid up. "Everyone's paid in full now. Thanks."

"Any old business?" Becky asked.

The phone rang, and everyone jumped.

Jess hesitated, then picked it up. "Hello . . . Twelve Candles Club."

Hi, Jess. It's me.

Sagging with relief, Jess whispered to the others, "It's my mom."

I wanted to be sure you have Santa Rosita Realty down for party-helping the Saturday after next, her mother said. We'll need all four of you, if possible, from 4:00 to 10:00. We're expecting well over a hundred people.

"Whoa, a hundred people?" Jess repeated.

Three sets of eyes bugged out at Jess.

Is that too many for you to handle? Mom asked. If it is, we can always get—

"Nope—it's not too many," Jess interrupted quickly. "We had almost that many at Mrs. Llewellyn's barbecue. And now we're experienced."

The girls nodded.

Good. Don't forget then.

"Cara will post it on the greenboard right now," Jess assured her mother. Cara was poised at the board as Jess repeated, "Santa Rosita Realty, Saturday after next, 4:00 to 10:00. Right?"

Correct. Everything okay at home?

"Uh—fine, I guess," Jess answered, not wanting to get into a discussion with her mother about anything right now. "We just got back from our clown birthday party."

That brings me to the second item, her mother continued. I have another job for all of you tonight. I've got the Neighborhood Watch meeting fliers distributed, and people will be coming to our house from 7:00 till 9:00. We need baby-sitters, but I can't tell you how many kids will be there.

"Let me ask the others," Jess said.

She quickly explained the job for tonight, and amazingly, everyone was available.

"Okay, Mom, we're on from 7:00 till 9:00 tonight."

Thank goodness. By the way, I have a wonderful surprise for you when I get home.

"A surprise? What is it?"

It wouldn't be much of a surprise if I told you, her mother teased.

"I guess not."

See you at dinnertime. Be careful.

Before Jess could respond, her mother had hung up.

Four phone calls followed for car washing, housecleaning, and baby-sitting. Luckily, everyone had good references.

When there was a break in the calls, Becky said, "Let's try again. Any old business?"

Tricia raised her hand. "My mom thinks we should use the Baby-sitting Safety Checklist that the police gave us. We could make copies to take with us every time we baby-sit. I brought mine with me."

Jess hadn't looked at hers, and grabbed it now from the top of her desk. "Let's read it," she said.

"It's all the stuff we should know," Cara said after they'd gone over the list, "but sometimes parents are in a hurry or the kids are crying, and we don't get the information. I motion that we always take a copy with us, get it filled out, and keep it near the phone. People will be impressed to see how organized we are."

No one objected, and the motion passed.

"Other stuff," Becky added. "If the phone rings while we're baby-sitting, we should never tell the caller we're alone. We can say we're visiting and the child's parents can't come to the phone right now, but we'll give them a message. If anyone gets rude, we should hang up. And, if anyone comes to the door, we should never open it, *never* say that we're baby-sitting."

Jess flopped down on the floor. "Okay, but I don't feel like discussing any problems right now." Sitting on the floor with her legs crossed Indian style, she did a leg pull.

Tricia plopped down on the floor beside Jess and did a leg pull herself. "We have to face trouble, Jess, not hide our heads in the sand like ostriches."

Baby-sitting Safety Checklist

ADDRESS AND PHONE: _____

_____

WHERE PARENTS WILL BE: _____

_____

EMERGENCY FRIEND OR RELATIVE: _____

CHILD(REN)'S DOCTOR: _____

ALLERGIES: _____

MEDICATIONS: _____

NIGHT LIGHT? _____

SPECIAL INSTRUCTIONS: _____

_____

_____

TIME EXPECTED TO RETURN: _____

SITTER'S CHARGE PER HOUR: _____

SITTER MUST BE HOME BY: _____

EMERGENCY EXITS IN CASE OF FIRE: _____

WHERE ARE FIRE EXTINGUISHERS? _____

HOW DO DOORS & WINDOWS LOCK? _____

OUTSIDE LIGHT ON? _____

POLICE: _____

FIRE DEPARTMENT: _____

RESCUE SQUAD: _____

POISON CONTROL CENTER: _____

Jess did the other leg, stretching out her muscles. "I wish everything were just the way it was the last day of school when we were at Becky's planning the club. We had so much fun."

"I do, too," Becky said. "But things aren't the same. They just aren't."

"I guess not," Jess answered, brushing her hair away from her face.

"Hey," Cara asked, "where did you get that old trunk by your back window?"

"Dad just inherited it from a great aunt in northern California," Jess answered. "Mom didn't think it went well with her southwestern decor, so I took it. My lazy brothers finally got around to carrying it in here last night."

"What about these old pictures lying on top?" Becky asked, crossing the room to the trunk.

"They came with it. I'm going to ask Dad to hang them."

The others joined Becky to look at the faded brown photographs. They were mounted in narrow wooden frames under cloudy glass. One photo was of a couple standing in front of a covered wagon with oxen. In another, the same couple stood with some kids in front of a log church.

"Who are these people?" Tricia asked.

"My great-great—I don't know how many times great—grandparents, Oakley and Elspeth McColl, and their four kids, who came to California during the Gold Rush," Jess answered.

"Did they find any gold?" Becky asked.

"I doubt it," Jess said. "Oakley McColl was the minister of that old log church."

"You're kidding!" Tricia said. "That means you have a minister in your family, too."

"A long time ago. I hadn't thought much about it until I got the pictures."

Cara squinted at the faded images. "Their names are printed below the photos. Hey, isn't Elspeth your middle name?"

"Yup. I was named for her," Jess admitted. "I used to hate it, but now that I've got their trunk and pictures, it's sort of interesting. Dad and my brothers are all middle-named Oakley. Dad told Mom she could first-name us whatever she pleased, but he wanted to keep Elspeth and Oakley in the family. That's probably why we inherited the trunk and stuff."

"Hmmm," Becky mused, looking up from the pictures to Jess. "You know, you look a lot like your Grandma Elspeth. In fact, if you'd wear your hair up in a knot like this, you'd look *just* like her. You'd make a good pioneer woman."

Jess laughed.

"Come on!" Tricia said. "Jess, a pioneer woman? Now I've heard everything!"

"I don't know," Jess objected. "Sometimes I feel . . . almost like two people. There's the old-fashioned side of me who loves the little flowered print of my bed comforters, and another side who has a gym for a bedroom!"

"I'm going to draw the pioneer side of you in a sunbonnet and flowered dress," Becky decided. "I'll put you in front of a covered wagon with oxen, just like this picture."

"I love it!" Jess said.

"Anything interesting, like old clothes, in the trunk?" Tricia asked.

Jess shook her head. "Only old books and stuff. Dad hasn't had time to really look through it yet."

"Any wonderful diaries or journals?" Cara asked. "Any juicy family secrets?"

"Letters, birth certificates, and stuff like that," Jess answered. Cara was always curious, probably because she wanted to be a writer, but she was sensitive enough not to be disgustingly nosey.

After a moment, Jess added, "It's all from Dad's family. Mom doesn't care for Bibles and stuff." She decided to change the subject. "Don't forget, you're all coming to my slumber party Sunday night, and we're going to have fun! It'll be the best slumber party ever, one we'll remember forever and ever."

Tricia gave her friend a sideways glance. "Let's just hope we can all come . . . and that it won't be *too* memorable!"

CHAPTER

5

In the family room, stacked chairs from Mom's office stood in rows. Jess counted them, plus the number of places to sit on the tan leather couches and chairs, and on the tiled seating area in front of the fireplace. "Forty," Jess said. "We can seat forty people."

"If more come," her mother said, "they can sit on the floor."

Jess read one of the bright yellow fliers Mom had distributed herself around the neighborhood:

> Are you aware of the attempted break-ins and robberies that have occurred in our area? If not, here's your chance to learn about them—and to do something to stop further crime.
>
> Tonight, a Crime Prevention Representative from the Santa Rosita Police Department will speak to those who

are interested in forming a Neighborhood Watch Program in Santa Rosita Estates.

We hope you will join us. Free child care (and pool lifeguarding) will be provided for your children. Be sure to bring their bathing suits if you want them to use the pool.

Do you know the best crime preventive device ever invented?

It's a good neighbor!

After the date, time, and their address, Mom had signed her name. Jess turned to her mother, who was wiping out two huge punch bowls. "What do you mean by attempted break-ins and robberies that have occurred in our area? Have there been lots of them?"

Mom tossed her head impatiently. "There've been other attempted break-ins, and there've also been robberies, but I didn't want to alarm you. Your ordeal was bad enough."

"Whose houses?" Jess asked, suspicious.

"Well," her mother began, "they've been mostly on Seaview Boulevard and the expensive houses along the ocean. You did mention that the O'Lone's had been robbed."

"But that's *not* Santa Rosita Estates," Jess argued.

Her mother's grayish-blue eyes met hers. "All of Santa Rosita is our neighborhood, young lady. What affects other parts of town will eventually affect us. It's best to start a Neighborhood Watch now and be prepared."

Jess suspected it was another of her mother's ways of "making herself available" as a realtor. Best not to mention it, though, or she'd be at the mercy of her mom's notorious temper.

Besides the two punch bowls, the kitchen counter was laden with trays, boxes of cookies, napkins and plastic glasses, and a brown paper bag. Mom pushed the bag toward Jess. "Here's something for the Twelve Candles Club to wear around their necks, so the children will know who's in charge."

"For us?" Jess asked, opening the bag.

"For you."

Jess pulled out four white ribbon necklaces, each with a small brass candle-shaped ornament attached.

"They're really Christmas tree ornaments," her mother explained, "but I thought they'd be perfect. It's like a trademark necklace for the club. It will help the kids know who's in charge."

Jess admired hers, slipping it around her neck. "Thanks!" Jess said sincerely. Mom always got her way, so why fight it? Besides, they were nice.

Her mother eyed the necklace against Jess's T-shirt. "It looks as good as I'd hoped. When you have a job, you have to do things that make you stand out more than the others. Remember that, Jess."

Jess couldn't help asking, "Like a realtor organizing a Neighborhood Watch?"

"Exactly," her mom answered, heading for the fridge. "Something to make people remember you later, when they need your services. As I recall, the Polka-dot Clowns gave out a clown coloring page with promotion information and your phone number after the first party."

"Right," Jess admitted. Mom had nailed her there.

Her mother took out frozen rings of lemonade for the punch bowls. "Any objections to my organizing a Neighborhood Watch?"

"I guess not. Thanks, Mom, for the necklaces."

Her mother smiled, then glanced at the kitchen wall clock. "Good grief! It's almost seven o'clock. Get the cookies, plastic glasses, and napkins out onto the patio. And hide the cookies under the tablecloth until eight-thirty, or the kids will gobble them up before you know what's happened."

"You're right about that," Jess agreed.

"I'm putting you in charge of answering the doorbell and getting people to put on their name tags," her mother added. "The tags are on the card table in the entry. Your father and I will be greeting the guests inside."

As usual, Mom had everything organized. Jess put the packs of napkins, plastic glasses, and boxes of cookies on the huge wooden patio tray.

"I almost forgot!" Mom exclaimed as the front doorbell rang. "Oh, dear—" She leaned over the kitchen sink to look out the window. "It's just your friends, thank goodness. You can give them the instructions. Tell your father to come here. You're in for a surprise."

Jess rushed to the patio screen door. "Dad!" she yelled, "Mom wants you in here!"

Her father raised a hand and nodded. He'd been discussing lifeguarding with Jordan and Mark, who were in their swim trunks. Garner had a date, escaping lifeguard duty tonight.

Jess rushed to the front door. "Come on!" she said, letting her friends in. "Everybody will be here any minute."

Tricia noticed the candle medallion around Jess's neck. "How cute! Where did you get the necklace?"

"Mom got one for each of us," Jess told them. She hurried them behind the spiral staircase to the family room. "She says they can be our trademark. Tonight, they'll make us stand out from the other kids."

"All right!" Becky said. "We can wear them to parties, too, like Mrs. Llewellyn's on Friday night."

"Thank goodness they're . . . discreet," Cara said, finding just the right word, as usual. "I don't feel like standing out in the crowd tonight—like a clown."

Tricia blinked at her. "Didn't you like being a clown?"

"Sure. For a while," Cara answered. "But I wouldn't want to be one every day."

"Hurry it up," Jess told them. "Get your candle necklaces on and let's set everything up for the kids outside. Everyone will be arriving any minute."

They tied on the white ribbons, and hurried out to the patio with the tray of cookies and lemonade. Jess had put a white imitation lace tablecloth over the glass-topped table, since Mom was sure the kids would be spilling punch everywhere.

The doorbell rang again, and Mom yelled, "Jess, get it!"

Jess ran through the house to open the door. A middle-aged man and woman stood staring at her. "Hello. I'm Jess McColl. I guess you're here for Neighborhood Watch."

"We're Mr. and Mrs. Merwich," the woman said. "We're house-sitting next door while the Herringtons are in Australia, but we thought we should come so we can report to them about the meeting." Mrs. Merwich had a round face, and her round glasses made her eyes look almost owlish. Mr. Merwich wore glasses, too, but his were thick as bottle glass, and he looked a little peculiar with bangs that hung down to his dark eyebrows.

Jess realized she was staring at them. "Ah . . . won't you come in, please? We have name tags for everyone on the card table. Then, if you'll go to the family room . . . It's behind the stairs to your right."

Just then, Mrs. Preskitt, who lived across the street, arrived at the door. She smiled, as friendly as ever. "Well, Jess, I see that your mother has put you to work."

"You know it," Jess said, directing her to the name tags and the family room.

Next, Tricia Bennett's mother arrived with Suzanne and Bryan. Behind them was Becky's mother, Mrs. Hamilton, and five-year-old Amanda. People began to stream through door, including Cara's parents, and Jess scarcely had time to greet them, let alone point out the name tags. She heard an excited squeal from the backyard, but there was no time to check it out.

Suddenly she saw Mr. and Mrs. Merwich—coming from the living room! *What are they doing in there?* Jess thought. "The family room is over here," she explained again, pointing to the right.

They stared at her owlishly and nodded.

What if they're casing the place? Jess thought. *What if they aren't really house-sitting next door? Maybe they just got a hold of one of Mom's invitations. . . .*

"Hello there, Jess," Mr. Terhune greeted her at the door. He was a tall, thin man—even his face was bony—but he had a nice smile. "I understand you'll be cleaning our house on Saturday."

"I guess so. Thanks for asking us again." She pointed out the name tags, then glanced back and saw that the Merwiches had disappeared, hopefully into the family room this time.

Another couple was at the door with two little girls for TCC to baby-sit. Behind them came more people with kids. And then a woman police officer arrived, who Jess guessed was the Crime Prevention Specialist.

By seven-thirty, the doorbell had stopped ringing, and it appeared that everyone was settled in the family room. Over the hum of voices, Jess could hear her mother announce, "I'm Alexis McColl, and that's my husband, Ben, coming in from organizing the children and lifeguards. We're glad you've come to learn about starting a Neighborhood Watch program. Welcome to our home."

Jess locked the front door and hurried to the family room. The seats were all filled, and some people sat at the breakfast counter on barstools.

Her mother was introducing Officer Cheryl Lane, the Crime Prevention Specialist, when Jess noticed that Mr. and Mrs. Merwich were outside, looking over the backyard.

Jess squared her shoulders and headed for the sliding screen door. She put on a good smile and told Mrs. Merwich, "The meeting is starting now."

"Oh," the woman said, her eyes growing even larger. "We were just admiring your lovely backyard and swimming pool."

Jess managed to keep on smiling.

As they stepped into the house, Mr. Merwich didn't return her smile. He almost appeared angry, his dark brows furrowed under his thick glasses.

From a kitchen barstool, Dad caught Jess's eye. He pointed at something outside, but she couldn't see what he meant.

The doorbell rang, and Jess was on her feet again. It was the Ashwells from down the street, late because of heavy traffic on the way home from work. Jess showed them the name tags and locked the front door again.

Wouldn't it be something if thieves came to a Neighborhood Watch meeting? she thought. *Or if a burglar was out robbing these people's houses right now?*

No one else was coming up the street, and Jess headed through the sliding screen door from the living room so as not to disturb the meeting. Outside, six kids were swimming under her brothers' watchful eyes. Her TCC friends were dancing the Hokey-Pokey with ten or eleven other kids. It was great to see how good they were at keeping the kids busy.

She wandered to the backyard wall near her room, and decided to stand up on a decorative rock. She could just barely see over the stucco wall. Nothing moved along the back hill or the sidewalk behind her room and the garage. At least not now. She jumped down.

When she looked up, Mr. Merwich was standing nearby watching her. He nodded, then strolled away. Maybe he was just nosey, but Jess didn't like it at all.

The doorbell rang again, and Jess raced inside.

It was Mr. and Mrs. Bay, from across the street. "We were watching the news, and forgot all about the meeting until we noticed all the cars," she explained.

Jess walked them to the family room and stopped to listen.

Officer Lane was saying, "Right now we think the explosion of thefts in Santa Rosita is related to a drug habit that's gone over the edge. This kind of drug addict often commits acts that don't make any sense—such as robbing in broad daylight without a disguise."

Jess drew a deep breath, listening intently.

"Neighbors working together with law enforcement can make one of the best crime-fighting teams around," Officer Lane said. "It requires neighbors getting to know one another and working together . . . citizens being trained to recognize and report suspicious activities . . . programs like Operation Identification, which engraves your valuables with your driver's license number. Window seals will identify you as an Operation Identification member. This helps deter theft, and aids police in the recovery of lost or stolen items. . . ."

Jess glanced around the room, and noticed Mr. Merwich staring at her again. Or was he? His glasses were so thick it was hard to tell. Behind her, she heard a scratch at the screen door. She turned. A puppy! A cute brown puppy that looked almost like a little bear. *Was that what all the squealing was about?* Jess thought.

Cara caught her eye from outside.

Whose dog is it? Jess mouthed, pointing at the puppy.

Cara pointed at her. *It's yours!* she mouthed back.

Jess jabbed a finger at herself. *Mine?*

Cara nodded.

So this was the surprise Mom had called Dad about! Sure, she'd want a dog now that a burglar was around, but would such a little puppy do much good? Still, he might bark.

Jess opened the screen door and sat down just outside, lifting the puppy to her lap. His big brown eyes looked up at her, and he wagged his tail. After a while, he lost interest and turned around, looking as though he wanted to get down but didn't know how. Jess laughed. He looked up at her, then somersaulted off her lap, landing in a four-legged split.

Tumbles, Jess thought. *I'll call him Tumbles—Tumbles Burglar-Catcher McColl.*

Inside, she could hear what Officer Lane was saying. "We like the neighbors to be informed of possible trouble. For example, we'd like all of you to be on the lookout for a battered blue van that was seen in front of this house at the time of the attempted car theft. Of course, the suspect may have stolen another vehicle by now."

Ufff! Jess thought. She should have expected it. *If only Officer Lane didn't have to mention the burglar and that miserable old van again!*

CHAPTER

6

The next morning was Wednesday, and Jess and Cara rode their bikes to the Bennetts' house for Morning Fun for Kids. "Let's hope-hope-hope the Funners aren't so wild today," Jess said.

"Right," Cara agreed. "Tricia said she had a plan."

"Another plan?" Jess asked. "Like what?" The first few mornings they'd had the four- to seven-year-old kids, or Funners, as they called them, things had been so frantic that Jess felt like giving up. The Funners, who came on Monday, Wednesday, and Friday mornings, still weren't too quiet or under control yet.

"Who knows what Tricia's dreamed up this time," Cara answered as they pulled their bikes into the Bennetts' driveway.

"I'll open the garage door to park our bikes," Cara said. She hopped off hers, and let herself through the breezeway gate.

The yellow poster on the breezeway gate was already up:

MORNING FUN FOR KIDS
PLEASE KNOCK ON GATE

What a pain to have to be so careful with our bikes now, Jess thought for the umpteenth time. She glanced down the street, but there was no sign of the blue van or any other suspicious-looking vehicle. So far, the only good that had come from the burglar trouble was Tumbles.

In a moment, Cara raised the garage door, and Jess rode her bike in. "We're expecting fifteen kids this morning," Cara told her.

"Yipes!" Jess exclaimed. "What ever made us think we could take care of all these kids, anyway?"

"We wanted to make some extra money, remember?" Cara said. "And especially because we didn't want Becky to move away."

In the fenced backyard, Becky was already setting out the craft supplies at the big redwood table. She wore a blue T-shirt that matched the color of her eyes.

She'd just finished stacking pink felt squares and setting out colored pens. "What's happening?" Jess asked her.

"We're making felt pictures today," Becky answered. "Maybe bookmarks, too, if we need to fill up more time."

"I meant what's happening with Tricia?" Jess said. "I hear she has something new for the kids today."

Becky pushed her long dark hair away from her face. "Mrs. Bennett says it's a secret, that we'll all see what she's up to as soon as the Funners arrive. In the meantime, the three of us will have to greet all the parents and handle the signing in of the Funners. Better check everything out now."

Jess glanced at the sign-in table. Name tags and pens were laid out, and a clipboard with forms for parents to fill in their child's name, age, time checked in and out, home phone, and doctor's name and phone. "All okay here," Jess announced.

Jess looked around the yard. There was a wooden play gym, a sandbox, and a tree house in the California pepper tree, all enclosed by a solid wooden fence. Butterscotch, the Bennett's old cat, sat in the kitchen window pass-through shelf, as usual. Jess hoped no one brought pet mice today, like Blake Berenson had brought last Friday. Jess also made sure there were no rakes, shovels, pruners, or other dangerous pointy things lying around in the yard. More important, there were no bad guys lurking around the other side of the fence. "Everything looks fine," she said to no one in particular.

Amanda Hamilton, Becky's little sister, came running out of the Bennetts' family room door with Suzanne and Bryan Bennett. "Almost time to start!" Suzanne, who was seven, announced. "What's the surprise?"

"Exactly what we're wondering," Jess said. "Don't you know, either?"

Suzanne shook her head. "Not me. Tricia wouldn't tell. And Mom says we're supposed to get the brown carpet from the garage for our magic carpet ride. Tricia wants us to roll it out and have all the Funners sitting on it, ready for the surprise."

Jess shrugged. "Then let's get the rug out."

Jess, Cara, and Becky carried out the old brown carpet and rolled it out across the patio. It was long and narrow with ragged edges. As soon as it was down the Funners started to arrive.

First came Jojo and Jimjim Davis with their cousin, who they called All-tarr. He had green eyes and freckles just like the twins.

"Is that really his name?" Jess asked.

Mrs. Davis smiled. "It's actually Alistair, but he couldn't pronounce it, so he's become All-tarr."

"Hello, All-tarr," Jess said. "I remember you from Jojo and Jimjim's birthday party."

"Were you there?" All-tarr asked.

Yipes! Jess thought. He'd only seen her as a clown, and clowns were never to reveal their true identity.

"Come on, boys," Jess said, changing the subject. "Let's get settled on the magic carpet. There's going to be a special surprise today. Here come some more Funners already."

Within minutes, all fifteen excited Funners sat squirming and poking each other on the brown carpet. "What's the surprise?" Craig Leonard asked with impatience.

"Yeh, what's the surprise?" others echoed.

"Umpty-dumpty-um-el-la-ump!" the Davis twins yelled with excitement. Then cousin All-tarr began to yell crazy stuff with them, trying to imitate their secret twin language.

Suddenly the faint sound of jingling came from the breezeway, growing louder and louder until Tricia-Jingles peeked around the corner in a green polka-dot clown suit and red yarn wig, complete with clown makeup.

"Good morning, Funners!" Tricia-Jingles said happily, hopping along and jingling. "I'm Jingles, the Clown. I've come to take you on a magic carpet ride to . . . guess where?"

The Funners sat wide-eyed on the brown carpet. "Where?" they yelled. "Where?"

"You have to guess, or we can't go," Jingles said.

"To a birthday party?" All-tarr Davis asked.

"No, not to a birthday party," Jingles answered, shaking her shaggy red wig.

"To the moon again?" someone asked.

"No," Jingles answered. "Clowns don't go to the moon. Where do clowns go?"

"To the circus!" Blake Berenson yelled.

"Hurray for Blake!" Jingles called out. "We're going to the circus! Now, all of you Funners move over a little so I can stand in the middle of the carpet. And you, Jessica Elspeth McColl, can do cartwheels all around us so we can take off for the circus properly!"

"Yes, sir, Jingles sir," Jess answered, then began to cartwheel around them on the rug. She might not get as much tumbling practice in her bedroom gym as she used to, but she sure got a lot of it working for the Twelve Candles Club.

When Jess was halfway around the circle, Jingles called out, "Okay, Funners, hold on to the corners and edges of our m-a-g-i-c c-a-r-p-e-t and close your eyes, then we'll z-o-o-m to the b-i-g t-o-p circus. R-e-a-d-y?"

"Ready!" they yelled. "Ready!" They scrunched their eyes shut and clung to the ragged edges of the rug.

Jingles flung out a jingly arm. "Harrruuummm . . . har-rruuummm. T-a-k-e o-f-f! T-a-k-e o-f-f! Here we go through the air! Remember to keep your eyes shut!"

Jess had to smile as she finished her cartwheels. Tricia might be a ham, but she sure knew how to hold the Funners' attention. It was amazing how all four of them in TCC had such different talents. Tricia and Becky claimed that God gave at least one talent to everyone, and that people just had to find theirs.

"Keep those eyes closed," Tricia-Jingles reminded them, "but in your imaginations, let's l-o-o-k b-e-l-o-w! Isn't that a huge circus tent? The big top! It's the big top! Let's circle down l-o-w-e-r and l-o-w-e-r. . . . Whoa! The clowns and animals and circus performers are just getting ready to go into the tent. The opening parade is ready to start! Listen to the trumpet and drum fanfare . . . and there's the ringmaster's whistle. *'Ladies and gentlemen . . . boys and girls of all ages, the circus will now begin!'* "

Even Jess could imagine the elephants, tigers, llamas, and circus performers parading around the outside ring in the big tent. And here came the clowns . . . riding on unicycles, in bathtubs, walking on stilts. . . .

"Question," Jingles said. "What did the ringmaster say when the human cannonball was shot out of the circus tent?"

Jingles answered herself: "That's going too far!" She laughed loudly, and the Funners laughed with her.

"Another question," Jingles said. "What do you call the dancing poodle when the elephant sits on him?"

"Flat!" someone guessed.

"Good guess! But that's not it," Jingles said.

The Funners guessed some more, but no one got it right.

"The underdog!" Jingles shouted, to the cheers of the kids.

Jingles succeeded at making everyone feel as if they were really in the circus tent. They saw the Oodles of Poodles act, the elephants' handstands, the lion tamers, and everything else. Finally, the trapeze artists came flying through the air. "Keep your knees together . . . knees together! It's a triple somersault in the air!" Jingles yelled.

The Funners yelled too, and pretended to eat cotton candy until it was time to fly back to Santa Rosita Estates. For the final leg of their journey, Jingles had them sing "Oom-pa-pa, oom-pa-pa" like an old-fashioned steam calliope.

When they opened their eyes, Tricia-Jingles was gone, and the Funners were sitting on the raggedy brown carpet alone.

"Where's Jingles?" the Funners yelled. "Where's Jingles?"

"Jingles has promised to come another time if you're good," Becky told them.

"We'll be good!" the Funners chorused solemnly. "We'll be very, very good."

After that they *were* good, not even spilling as much of their apple juice, or crumbling their graham crackers. At craft time, they drew pictures of clowns on their felt squares. It was the best Morning Fun for Kids yet, and Jess wished the kids were always that good.

When it was almost time for the parents to collect the Funners, Jess remembered something. "Where're the promotional coloring-picture handouts?" she asked Becky.

"At home in my room," Becky answered.

"We should be handing them out to the new parents," Jess said. "The Funners will all be talking about Jingles and going to the circus."

"You're right," Becky said. "Take care of the craft group, and I'll go home and get them."

When Becky returned from next door with the fliers, she said, "I also grabbed copies of 'A Clown's Prayer' for you and Cara. Tricia and I learned it at Clown School."

Jess looked at the paper decorated with colorful balloons, and the artistically lettered title. She began to read:

Dear Lord, help me create more laughter than tears, give more happiness than gloom, spread more cheer than despair.

Never let me grow so important that I don't see the wonder in the eyes of a child or the twinkle in the eyes of the aged.

Never let me forget that I am a clown . . . that my job is to cheer people up and let them forget, for a few moments, the unpleasant things in their lives.

Never let me grow so rich that I no longer call on my Creator in the hour of my need or fail to thank Him in my hours of plenty. Amen.

"I never thought about clowns praying," Jess said.

Becky smiled. "A lot of them do. A lot of them are Christians. That's why they're so joyful."

———

Later, when Jess returned home, the blinking red light on her answering machine greeted her. She could almost imagine the messages—a couple of hang-ups from weirdos, and a few clients for the Twelve Candles Club. It'd been such a good morning that Jess decided not to spoil it by listening to anything negative on the machine. Besides, she had to eat fast and get off to gymnastics practice. She could catch the messages later. Much later.

Right after lunch Dad drove her to the California Gold Gym, where she always worked out. In the dressing room, she changed into her favorite teal-green leotard.

When she came out into the gym, her dad was sitting in the corner, where he'd probably watch her for a while, then leave for his tennis game and pick her up later. She shot him a grin, and he grinned back. Starting her floor warm-ups, Jess tried to see the gym through her dad's eyes.

The building was shaped like a huge cube, and the sun streaming in through the skylights gave it an eerie other-worldly appearance. Most of the floor was covered with blue mats like those in her room, and several rings hung from the ceiling. At the far end were the vaulting horses, and to the left sets of parallel bars and uneven parallels. Near her dad, there were low balance beams for beginners; medium high, and higher beams beyond. The gym was busy as usual—girls were talking to one another and to the coaches, but most of them were running their routines, focusing on every step.

Once she'd finished her warm-ups, she lined up behind the other girls for her first vault. Coach Wheeler was spotting the vaulters, shoveling them over if they goofed. It seemed to take forever to move up.

Jess stepped forward, watching the girl in front of her run and vault. A good one!

Now she was up. Jess stood at the edge of the eighty-foot runway and concentrated on the vaulting horse at the other end. In a real gymnastics competition, she'd want to try to score a perfect ten on her vault like Mary Lou Retton had in the Olympics. But, as Coach Wheeler always said, you have to do a lot of tens in practice before you can do one in competition.

Jess shook her arms and legs, loosening her muscles. She blew a breath up her face and jogged in place, trying to calm her nerves. She'd nail this vault. *Nail it*. After all, vaulting was her best event. She squared her shoulders and narrowed her eyes. She'd go for it to show her dad that she was getting better.

"Nail it, Jess!" Coach Wheeler called out.

Ready, she raised her arm, then exploded down the runway, hitting the springboard like a jackhammer. She twisted into a handstand over the vault, her fingers barely brushing the leather as she launched into a full twist, then the layout back somersault and, still soaring, the half twist.

For an instant, Jess's mind flashed back to the burglar . . . and the instant ruined everything. Coach Wheeler's hands reached out to save her from a complete disaster, but she still whammed onto the blue gymnastics mat.

"Ohhh!" Jess moaned in pain and aggravation.

"What's wrong?" Coach Wheeler asked.

"Lost my concentration," she grumbled, pulling herself up. Her rear-end sure hurt, but her muscles were all right and no bones were broken.

"I know you lost your concentration," he said, concerned. "My question is why?"

Jess muttered, "We've had a burglar messing around our house, and some other scary stuff, and it's thrown me a little."

"I'm not surprised," he said. "Try it again, Jess. You've got fantastic power, but without perfect concentration, it won't be enough."

Jess nodded. She knew she had the power and determination to win. She'd won plenty of regional and even a few state competitions. That's why she had all those ribbons and trophies. But without perfect concentration . . .

Drawing a deep breath, Jess headed for the vaulting line again. One of the newer girls raised her hand, then raced down the runway. She hit the springboard hard, then twisted into a handstand just over the vault and came down on her feet on the gym mat.

"Good job," Coach Wheeler said. "A few more like that and we'll start to add twists and somersaults."

Jess let out a discouraged sigh. She'd done those beginning

runs over and over before she could even try the exciting stuff she did now. After so much work, she sure wasn't going to allow a stupid burglar to ruin everything. This time she'd be all power, determination, and concentration. This time she'd nail it.

She pictured every detail of her routine in her mind. The run-up held the first key, then to really jackhammer that springboard with power—

Sudden thoughts interrupted. *What I wouldn't do to catch that burglar myself! The Twelve Candles Club is going so well; in fact, everything would be fine if it weren't for that creep.*

No, no, forget about him! she thought. *Forget him, and do this vault right—like Mary Lou Retton, a perfect ten. Show Dad I can do it.*

Jess raised her hand, then raced down the runway. She hit the springboard like a jackhammer again, but the moment she went over the vault into her twist, she knew that it would be far from perfect. That dumb burglar was ruining everything!

CHAPTER

7

Jess laid her head back against the car seat as her dad drove down Ocean Avenue.

"You're awfully quiet, Jess," he remarked. "How'd the rest of gymnastics go?"

She puffed out a discouraged sigh. "I kept losing my concentration thinking about that no-good burglar. I tried over and over to put him out of mind, but I couldn't. Even Coach Wheeler saw that something was bothering me."

Her father kept an eye on the traffic. "It's bothering me, too, Jess. I like to think I can take care of my family, but when someone comes in uninvited, the situation can get out of control."

"Tricia says it has to do with evil," Jess remarked bluntly.

"It could," her father answered. "It certainly could."

"We don't talk about evil in our family," Jess said uneasily.

"Maybe we should," Dad answered.

As they drove into Santa Rosita Estates, Jess looked out the window. It was a cheery, well-kept neighborhood, one that looked like it wouldn't have any troubles. Evil seemed far away—like somewhere out in the ghettos.

"You working tonight?" Dad asked.

"Nope, there's just the TCC meeting at four-thirty. We clean for Mrs. Llewellyn tomorrow morning, though."

Dad smiled at her, then looked around the neighborhood himself. "There's Neighborhood Watch in action."

Jess saw Mrs. Bay walking along with her poodle. "She really is watching, huh, Dad? Whoa . . . there's that Mr. and Mrs. Merwich, the people who are supposedly house-sitting for the Herringtons. You know, last night they wandered into our living room after I told them that the family room was the other way. Then I caught them out looking over the backyard after the Neighborhood Watch meeting had started. I forgot to tell you."

"Probably just nosey because they're outsiders," her dad said. "Still, we should keep an eye on anyone who acts peculiar. It's nothing new. Evil's been around since the Garden of Eden."

"I don't like watching," Jess muttered. "I don't like not trusting people."

"I'm sure no one does," Dad said as he drove up their driveway. As usual, he parked the old white Toyota in the space behind the garage, and they could see right away that there was no one behind the garage or her room.

"Hey, let's see what's inside that trunk we inherited," her father said as they climbed out of the car. "I'd like to know more about old Oakley and Elspeth McColl. How about you?"

Jess nodded. "I guess so, since we're both middle-named for them."

"It's a date," her father answered. "I'll start going through some of the papers right away. I can take a load up to my office so I don't disturb your club meeting."

"You just don't want to get roped into washing cars or windows," Jess teased.

"You're right about that," Dad agreed, grinning, as Jess unlocked her front door.

"You keep it mighty dark in here," her father remarked.

"I didn't used to," she replied, opening the front mini-blinds.

"You mean BB, 'before burglar'?"

"Yeah, BB." The red blinking light on her answering machine caught Jess's attention. "Oh-oh, more messages."

"Let's hear them," her father said.

Jess moved the function selector to messages, and the tape clunk-clunk-clunked into position.

"*Grrraaahhh!*" someone growled. "*Grrraaahhh!*" Then came the familiar click as the caller hung up.

"See, Dad?" Jess moaned.

"Sounds like kids playing a prank," her dad said. "If we weren't looking for a burglar, it would almost be funny."

"They don't always growl," Jess said. "Sometimes they just hang up. One guy asked Cara about the Twelve Candles Club, and after she'd told him about it he hung up."

After the prank call, there were three messages for baby-sitting and car-washing jobs.

"I'll call the detective and let him know that the phone calls haven't stopped," her father said. "Why don't you open that back blind and let some more light in? We'll get started on the trunk before your friends arrive."

Jess squared her shoulders and headed to the back window.

She peered through the slats. Nothing new. This burglar business was making her furious, and for the first time in ages, she pulled the blind all the way up. The flood of sunshine soothed her anger.

As her father spoke to the police, Jess set aside the faded brown photographs of Oakley and Elspeth McColl, and opened the creaking lid of the trunk. Just the same old stuff. It was filled almost to the top with papers, bound certificates, and old books.

At last, Dad hung up the phone and came over to join her. "Nothing to report on the case."

"Figures."

"Maybe no news is good news," he said. He looked into the trunk with her. "Well, what have we here?"

"Bibles?" Jess asked.

"Yes. One has Oakley's name in it and the other apparently belonged to Elspeth. I shouldn't be surprised, since Oakley was a minister, but it is amazing when I consider what happened on my way home yesterday."

"What's that?"

"On the flight from Singapore, I ran into an old college friend on the plane. We got to talking, and I found out he's become a minister. I had been worried about all of you on this trip for some reason—before I'd heard about the burglar, of course. Anyway, I told my friend that I was worried about my family."

Jess stared at her father. "What did he say?"

Her father raised his grayish-brown brows, and a tender look filled his eyes. "He said he'd pray for me—for all of you. And he did, right there on the plane. When he finished, I wasn't worried anymore. It was the strangest thing. I felt like you were all in God's hands . . . and I hadn't thought about God for years, probably not since my Sunday school days."

"You went to Sunday school?" Jess asked.

"I did, but your mother doesn't like to hear me talk about it, so I've never said much."

Just then Jess heard voices out front. "Order in the court, the clowns want to speak!" her friends chanted. "Speak, clowns, speak! Order in the court—"

"Sounds like it's time for your meeting," her dad said, grabbing a box of papers from the trunk. "I'll take this stuff with me. See you later, kiddo."

"This meeting of the Twelve Candles Club will now come to order," Becky announced from her usual perch on the desk chair. The others sat on the twin beds. "Any old business?"

Cara nodded, looking embarrassed. "I messed up. I can't baby-sit Saturday night because I'll be in L.A., and I said I'd sit for my old regulars, the Stallings' girls."

"I'll be in L.A., too," Tricia put in.

"And I'm sitting for Jojo and Jimjim," Becky explained.

"That leaves me," Jess said reluctantly. They all knew she didn't care much for baby-sitting because she didn't have much experience at it. "I guess I can do it."

"Hey, thanks!" Cara said. "They're close by and easy to take care of . . . I guess I should tell you, though . . ."

"Tell me what?" Jess asked.

Cara drew a deep breath. "Last week when I sat for them . . . I had a feeling that someone was watching me through the back windows. They don't have drapes or blinds in the family room."

"Now you tell me!" Jess grumbled.

"Just put the back yardlight on when it gets dark," Cara

told her. "The Stallings don't stay out real late anyway."

"Sounds like fun-fun-fun," Jess mumbled, shaking her head. Then she went straight for her trampoline to jump away her nervousness.

"You're not the only one," Becky said. "I felt like I was being watched, too, when I stayed with Jojo and Jimjim. I forgot to close the drapes before it got dark, and, believe me, I won't do that again. I prayed like anything."

"Come on," Tricia complained. "Let's not get spooked out. It's important to be careful, but we can't let fear rule us. Perfect love casts out fear."

Jess jumped faster on the trampoline. "Explain, please."

"Well . . . if you love God, then He's in you and protects you," Tricia told her.

In you? Jess wondered, still jumping on the trampoline. As for loving God, she'd never thought about it. How could anyone love someone they couldn't see? She darted a glance at Cara, who looked puzzled, too. Best to change the subject. "Before I forget, do you all have permission to come to my slumber party Sunday night?"

Cara shook her head forlornly. "I haven't asked yet. I thought if things calmed down about that burglar, I'd have a better chance of getting permission. As it is, my father's barely letting me stay in this club."

"I'll be here for the slumber party," Tricia promised.

Becky raised a hand. "Me, too. Now, is there any other old business?"

"We still don't have a clown-promotion video," Cara said. "Maybe we can bring our clown outfits to the slumber party. That is, *if* I can come. Jess could do gymnastics, and we could do a few skits. I could videotape it like a play. It might even be better than a video showing us at a real birthday party when we're so busy with the kids."

"I make a motion that we bring our clown suits to Jess's slumber party Sunday night," Tricia said.

Cara nodded. "Seconded. *If* everyone can come."

During the it's-been-moved-and-seconded, Jess climbed up on her balance beam to try a stag leap, which wasn't easy. It took a lot of balance.

"Now that we've been a club for a few weeks," Becky said, "I think we need to know how everyone feels about it."

"It's g-r-e-a-t for me," Tricia answered right away. "I get a chance to act for an audience, and I like making my own money so I can buy things—like my new one-inch heels. And it's special, too, being able to give my own offering money at church."

No one else spoke up, so Jess said, while balancing along on the beam, "I like it because . . . I'm getting to know all of you better, not just the kids at gymnastics practice and meets. And I like making my own money, too." She did a stag leap into the air, then landed on the beam perfectly.

The phone rang, and Jess muttered, "Let's hope it's not another—" She decided not to say *weirdo*, but everyone knew what she meant.

They all stared at the phone, and finally Tricia grabbed it. "Twelve Candles Club." She listened, then flashed them a thumbs-up sign. "Yes, I'm sure that someone will be available to baby-sit for you Monday night, Mrs. Terhune. May I call you back in a few minutes?"

Jess jumped from the balance beam down to her trampoline and began to bounce. "There's no way I'd take that job—not with a new baby!"

"I'd be glad to take it," Tricia said. "I love babies."

"Tricia Bennett, you're crazy," Cara said.

"Only a little," Tricia answered. "Anyhow, I'm more used to babies because of having a little brother and sister in my own family."

After that, the phone didn't stop ringing. It was all they could do to keep the job offers sorted out, and Cara was busy chalking them up on the greenboard. Then Tricia did the callbacks. It took until after five-thirty to get everything worked out, and their jobs entered in each of their daily-planner calendars.

"Wacko!" Tricia said as they were leaving. "Club El Wacko is out of control!"

Becky laughed. "With lots and lots of jobs. Just what we wanted! Phooey on the burglar, and three cheers for the Twelve Candles Club!"

—————

At the dinner table, Jess's dad zapped off the TV with the remote control, probably because the news was full of burglaries, murders, and other awful stuff. "I'd like us to begin saying grace before we eat our meals," he announced.

Everyone tensed up.

"We're going to pray?" Garner asked. "Since when?"

"Since today," his dad said.

Mom shot him a shocked look. "Really, Ben, we haven't even discussed this."

Dad leaned over and dropped a kiss on her cheek. "Let's pray, and we'll talk later. The kids are all old enough to be part of something this important."

Jordan jumped up from the table.

"Where are you going, Jordo?" Dad asked.

"Ummm—I need mayo for the enchiladas."

"Fine. We'll all sit here and wait for you."

"The Mayo Kid strikes again!" Jess joked, then wished she hadn't because everyone looked so edgy.

"Really, Ben . . . prayer!" Jess's mom said unhappily.

"*Really*, my dear. I think it's high time for this family to turn over a new leaf."

"I like the old leaf just fine," she objected.

Jess's dad thought a moment, then said slowly, "I've recently realized that I didn't like it much anymore. I began to hope there was more to life."

Mom drew an impatient breath. "I suppose next you'll want us to hold hands while you pray."

"Might not be a bad idea," he answered.

Mom let out a loud "Hmmmph!"

Jess couldn't believe this was happening. At least she'd had some warning when Dad mentioned his college friend praying for them on the plane.

Everyone darted looks at their father until Jordan returned with the mayo. Usually nothing bothered him, but Jordan's face was nearly as red as his curly hair.

"Shall we bow our heads and pray?" Dad suggested calmly.

Jess bowed her head, wondering about the others, but determined not to look.

"Dear Heavenly Father," her dad began. "You haven't heard much from this family, and I'm sorry about that. I feel as if it's my fault. I ask for your forgiveness, and promise that things are changing. We thank you for this food and your blessing upon it. We thank you for our fine family, and for the many blessings we've taken for granted. We ask that you would protect this family from danger. We pray in the name of your Son, Jesus Christ. Amen."

Everyone looked up at him, and Dad smiled sheepishly. "I'm not much good at praying, but I can learn," he said. "I expect God is pleased to hear from me anyhow."

Mom tried not to show how flustered she felt as she passed the salad. "I suppose you'll be wanting to go to church."

"As a matter of fact, I was hoping you'd all join me Sunday morning at the Santa Rosita Community Church, where my old college friend, Don Wirt, is the minister. I met him yesterday on the flight home."

Jess watched her brothers' eyes nearly pop from their sockets, and her mother slap a spoonful of rice onto her plate with a loud CLANG.

Her mother's voice turned harsh. "I thought we'd decided years ago to let the children make up their own minds about religion."

"We did. But it recently occurred to me that by not taking them to church, we've given them no choice at all. We're offering no faith . . . or no faith. We've shown them no alternative to combat the evil in the world today."

Mom's gray-blue eyes flashed. "I know where this is coming from—that old ugly trunk you inherited from the preacher Oakley McColl and his wife."

Dad raised his brows and shook his head. "Maybe the trunk has had some degree of influence, but meeting Don Wirt on the plane was a real eye opener to me. Most of all, I think God is bringing circumstances together to reveal himself to us. The fact is," he paused, looking at each member of his family, "I have rededicated my life to Christ."

Mom looked ready to leap up from her chair, but restrained

herself. "I should have known this would be coming eventually—first you insisted on being married in a church, and then when the children were born you insisted on middle-naming them Oakley and Elspeth!"

"Now, Alexis," he soothed her. He smiled and patted her shoulder until she settled back in her chair. "This doesn't mean I love any of you any less; if anything, I love each one of you more than ever. The love I feel now is different, more joyful than I've ever known before."

Mom stared at him uneasily, and Jess didn't know whether her mother was going to scream or cry.

Jess took a bite from her enchilada, but could scarcely swallow it. Between the burglar and the creepy phone calls, and now her dad's sudden return to . . . to being a Christian, it felt as if her life wasn't just turning wacko. It was getting way out of control.

CHAPTER

8

The next morning, Jess stopped her bike in front of Cara's house across the street. "Cara!" she yelled just as her friend opened the garage door and rode her bike out. Then Jess sang out, "Hi-ho, hi-ho, to Mrs. L.'s we go."

Cara grinned. "You're singing already?"

"More like squawking, this early," Jess admitted.

"Any more weirdo phone calls?" Cara asked as they pedaled down her driveway toward the street.

"None since yesterday, thank goodness."

They were dressed alike in white T-shirts, jean shorts, and white tennies, and it made Jess feel closer to Cara. Not that they were as close as Becky and Tricia, but they knew each other from school and from being neighbors. It was hard to make best friends when you were into gymnastics.

Cara pedaled alongside Jess. "What are the police going to do about the phone calls?"

Jess shrugged. "Nothing yet, I guess. We thought about asking the telephone company for a new phone number, but that'd wreck everything. Our clients already know our phone number. Besides, Dad says we shouldn't back down from evil . . . to be careful, but not to give in to it."

Cara didn't answer, but shot her a curious look.

Jess wasn't sure how she felt about it herself. "Remind me to discuss the phone calls at our meeting this afternoon."

"If *I* don't forget," Cara said, looking up at the hill behind Jess's house.

"Have you asked yet about coming to my slumber party Sunday night?"

Cara shook her head. "I'm not asking until we get home Sunday afternoon. That's my best chance. I can say Becky and Tricia are going to be there, and it's *just* across the street."

"Let's hope it works," Jess answered. "It wouldn't be a real slumber party with one of us missing."

Cara smiled gratefully. "I guess not."

Once their houses were behind them, Jess said, "Something else sort of strange happened."

"What?" Cara asked, riding beside her.

"My dad's a Christian—again."

Cara stared at her in disbelief. "I didn't know you could *stop* being a Christian."

"Maybe I said it wrong," Jess replied. "He went to church when he was our age, but I guess he didn't understand much then. He said they never talked about having a relationship with Jesus, you know, like Him being a real friend."

"A *real friend*?" Cara repeated.

Jess nodded. "It beats me. All I know is my dad wants us to pray before meals now, and even go to church with him on Sunday."

"Are you going?" Cara asked.

"Maybe I'll try it. I'd like to know what it's all about anyhow."

"What about praying before meals?" Cara asked.

"He prayed last night before dinner, but he was already gone before breakfast. Anyhow, I don't know anything about praying. Would you believe he went to a men's Bible study at six-thirty this morning? Mom thinks he's gone wacko."

"What do you think?" Cara asked.

Jess braked her bike between Tricia's house and Becky's. "I don't know. He seems sort of happy—you know, joyful. And he says he loves us even more than before."

Just then, Tricia opened the garage door and came riding out on her bike. She was wearing a white T-shirt, too, and it really set off her strawberry-blond hair. "Morning-o, club-os!" she called to them. "Beck-o phoned. She overslept. She'll catch up with us on the way."

Mrs. Bennett stepped into the garage from the house. "Good morning, ladies. Have fun!"

They waved and rode on down the street.

"Hey, Jess," Tricia said, "have you looked in that old trunk yet?"

"Yeh, Dad and I did," Jess answered.

"Find anything interesting?"

Jess slowed down to let Tricia catch up. "I looked at old Elspeth's Bible before I went to bed. You know what she wrote on the inside back cover?"

Tricia's green eyes filled with interest. "What?"

Jess tried to remember it exactly. "Something like, 'I can do all things through Christ, which strengtheneth me.' Do you know what that means?"

"It's a Bible verse," Tricia answered. "It means you can do everything God asks you to with the help of Christ, who gives you the strength and power to do it."

"Power?" Jess asked. "You mean like power for your body?"

"Yep. Strength in your character and physical power. When I need help, that's the verse I remember. I can do *anything* He wants me to do if I just ask, 'Jesus, please help me!' "

Jess mulled it over. "I wonder why Grandma Elspeth wrote it in her Bible if it's already in there anyway."

"Lots of people write down verses that mean a lot to them," Tricia replied. "Life must have been scary during the Gold Rush days. What else did she write in there?"

"Nothing else on the inside cover, but lots on the inside pages," Jess answered. "I thought the Bible was supposed to be holy, not *written* in."

"There's nothing wrong with writing down what a person's learned from the verses," Tricia said. "I think God is pleased when a person does that. It probably means they're serious about their faith."

Cara had been riding along quietly until now. "Jess said her dad's become a Christian," she blurted.

Tricia's mouth dropped open, then she beamed. "G-r-e-a-t! Great-great-great! Wow, that is so awesome!"

Jess took a moment for her friend's reaction to sink in. "I guess I'll be going to your church with him next Sunday."

"Really? Wait till Becky hears!" Tricia exclaimed. "We've been praying—"

Just then, it was time to cross Ocean Avenue, so the girls rode single file in the bike lane. *I can do all things through Christ, which strengtheneth me*, Jess thought, trying to make it stick in her brain. It seemed like a good thing to know.

Becky finally caught up to them, bringing up the rear in the bike lane until they turned onto Seaview Boulevard. They rode hard down the tree-lined street to avoid being late.

Just before nine o'clock, they arrived at Mrs. Llewellyn's ultra-modern, white stucco house and parked their bikes in the usual place behind her garage.

"There you are, girls!" Mrs. Llewellyn called in her excited, squawky voice. She was leaning precariously from an upstairs window. "Am I glad to see you! Wait till you hear what's happened! Let yourselves in the laundry room door; Mr. L. said he'd leave it open for you."

They trooped past the swimming pool, then through the laundry room, where Jess spotted piles of folded sheets and towels on the washer and dryer. "May as well carry these up," she said. Mrs. Llewellyn's regular cleaning lady was still sick, and the Llewellyns sent their laundry out to be done. TCC changed the sheets and cleaned the whole huge house on Thursday mornings.

Lulu Llewellyn, a red cocker spaniel, bounded downstairs to meet them in the party room.

"Been chasing any more pepperoni down Ocean Avenue?" Becky asked the dog, referring to her now-famous chase that had appeared on the TV news.

Lulu gave a doggy smile and thumped her stubby tail.

"I do believe she's ready for another chase," Tricia said. "Just look at her eyeing our bikes through the window."

"Come on," Jess said, "let's get our marching orders."

"Here I am, girls," Mrs. Llewellyn called as she hurried into the kitchen, stiff-legged as a bird. She wore a shocking pink silk robe that set off her frazzled red hair, and, as usual, she was slightly out of breath.

"Good morning, Mrs. L.," Jess said with the others.

"Good morning!" Mrs. Llewellyn exclaimed, which was usual since she never spoke in a normal tone. She scrutinized them through her thick glasses, which magnified her already huge eyes. "My, don't you all look bright and cheery! It's such a joy having you girls in my home, and taking on such a huge responsibility, too."

She wore high-heeled pink slippers, and steadied herself against the stainless steel island in the middle of the enormous kitchen. "Now, there are some nutritious breakfast muffins and all-fruit jam on the counter. Help yourself. I know you've probably had breakfast at home, but you've no doubt ridden off half your energy on the way over here."

Hardly pausing for breath, she went on, "You know, girls, if we'd kept our chauffeur, we could be sending him to pick you up, instead of your having to ride in that dangerous traffic down Ocean Avenue."

"Did you have a chauffeur?" Cara asked.

"We did," Mrs. Llewellyn answered, "but it's so hard to keep reliable help that we decided to give up having one. That's one of the reasons why I appreciate you girls so much—you're reliable."

Jess set her pile of sheets and towels on the stainless steel counter. It was best to listen and to do exactly what Mrs. L. told them, since she always ended up having things done her way. Mr. L. claimed that his wife was "hard to resist."

While they helped themselves to date-bran muffins and jam, Mrs. L. found her clipboard with two pages of instructions. "You'll never believe what happened!" she confided excitedly. "You know the dinner party for eight tomorrow night that I needed two of you for? Well, the most wonderful opportunity presented itself . . . it just simply fell into my lap."

Uh-oh! Jess thought. Her eyes met Becky's, and she knew Becky was uh-ohing in her head, too.

Mrs. L. rushed on. "A wonderful pianist is coming to play for us, so we're having twenty-four guests instead of eight. Now I'll need all four of you to help serve, if you can. It'll be a sit-down dinner, of course."

"It sure sounds different from your western barbecue with the country band," Jess said.

Mrs. L. laughed. "I do hope so!"

"Ah, Mrs. Llewellyn," Tricia began, "both Cara and I will be in Los Angeles. We can't help you tomorrow."

"Oh, dear, I'd forgotten!" the woman said, flapping her clipboard distractedly. "I am getting so forgetful! Well, maybe Wurtzel Catering can provide some extra help. Just so they're not like Mrs. Wurtzel," she said under her breath. "She's a wonderful cateress, but a terrible grump."

The girls must have looked uneasy, because Mrs. Llewellyn quickly added, "It'll all work out! Don't worry, it always does!"

Jess hoped she was right. They were never quite sure what to expect with Mrs. L. in charge.

———

On Friday, Jess helped with Morning Fun for Kids, practiced her gymnastics, then had Becky in for their TCC meeting. Cara and Tricia had already left for Los Angeles, so it was only the two of them. For a change, there were only a few phone calls.

Before they knew where the day had gone, Jess's father was driving them up the Llewellyns' circular driveway and dropping them off by the front door in their white skirts and blouses. They wore their candle medallions around their necks.

"Have fun!" Jess's dad called to them as he drove off.

"We'll try!" Jess answered.

"Ufff!" Becky sighed. "There's Mrs. Wurtzel's black catering van parked by the garage. I hope we can cheer her up!"

At the huge double-door entry, Jess pressed the doorbell. They could hear the chimes pealing through the house.

A moment later, Mrs. Wurtzel answered the door. She wore a black dress with a small white apron, and her black hair was pulled back into a knot behind her head. She looked as stern as ever, and if she didn't look like she might bite their heads off, Jess would have burst out giggling.

"Well!" Mrs. Wurtzel huffed. "Don't you girls know enough to come around to the kitchen door? Yer hired help, not guests! And don't forget it."

"Sorry," Jess managed.

"I hope you'll forgive us," Becky added.

Mrs. Wurtzel gave her a steely look, let out an exasperated "Hmmmphhh!" and opened the door for them. As they passed by her, Jess could sense the woman inspecting what they wore, then heard her comment, "You might've at least worn hose instead of them anklets."

"Hose?" Becky said. "We don't have hose yet, and we thought white anklets and sandals would be better than tennies."

"Hmmmph!" Mrs. Wurtzel said again between pursed lips. "And what're them crazy candles hangin' on yer necks?"

"They're candle medallions," Becky answered. "Jess's

mother gave them to us to show that we are members of the Twelve Candles Club."

Jess cleared her throat loudly, but it sounded more like a "Hmmmph" before Mrs. Wurtzel could let out another one.

Mrs. Wurtzel eyed Jess suspiciously. "Hurry along. There's plenty to do. I brought along a server who knows about doin' things right. See you pay attention to her."

They followed the cateress through the enormous entry adorned with huge plants and modern sculptures, and for tonight, two round tables covered with peach-colored tablecloths. There was a silver vase on each with fresh roses, sparkling china, sterling silver, and crystal goblets. Through the living room, Jess could see another table set for eight in the library, and the usual dining room table was set elegantly as well. Everything looked perfect, and Jess fervently hoped she and Becky wouldn't do anything to ruin it.

"We're servin' *Chicken Cordon Bleu*," Mrs. Wurtzel announced as they made their way to the kitchen. "Don't guess you girls know what it is."

Becky smiled politely. "It's ham and swiss cheese wrapped in a chicken breast."

"Hmmmph!" Mrs. Wurtzel managed.

"My mom likes to cook," Becky explained. "She made it Saturday night when Mr. Bradshaw came over for dinner."

Arriving in the kitchen, Mrs. Wurtzel held her chin high. "This here's my daughter-in-law. Call her Em."

Em looked like a younger version of Mrs. Wurtzel. She stirred a huge pot of steaming sauce. She looked at the girls with a frown that matched her dreary black dress. Except for long bangs, her dark hair was stretched into a severe knot at the back of her head, just like her mother-in-law's. She nodded, and said a quiet "Hello."

"Hi, I'm Jess."

"And I'm Becky . . . glad to meet you."

Em kept stirring, the perspiration streaming down her face. The ovens were on and the kitchen was very hot.

"I'll do the stirrin', Em," Mrs. Wurtzel said to her daughter-in-law. "Mrs. Llewellyn wants you to train 'em how to serve tables. They don't know nothin'."

Em frowned again as she led the girls into the entry. She blew a puff of air up at her bangs before she spoke. "First, we serve crab spread and crackers on the patio. That's easy. Then, just before dinner, you fill the water goblets on the tables with ice cubes and water. These two tables in the entry are yer responsibility. Ain't no carpet here, so if you spill water, don't break yer neck slippin' on this marble. When the guests are seated, serve 'em salad, then the main dish. After a while you can serve 'em dessert and coffee."

There was lots more to serving a sit-down dinner than Jess had imagined, and the doorbell was already ringing. "How did we ever get into this?" she whispered to Becky.

"Easy," Becky whispered back. "We told Mrs. L we'd help with a dinner for *eight* people, remember?"

Mr. Llewellyn, a short, gray-haired man, hurried down the stairs. "Good evening, girls. I'll get the door."

Mrs. L. bustled down right behind her husband, wearing a flowered dress sprinkled with bright sequins. "Don't you girls look fresh! And those candle medallions are exquisite!" she exclaimed. "It'll be a wonderful evening—just *wonderful*! I know it!"

"Quick," Em whispered to the girls, "back to the kitchen.

And don't be starin' at the guests."

Minutes later, Jess carried out a dish of crab spread, surrounded by crackers. She set it on one side of the glass-topped patio table. On the other side was a huge bowl of punch and little glass punch cups. Becky carried out bowls of pecans.

Mrs. Llewellyn escorted her friends to the patio. "We've kept it all rather simple because the party grew at the last minute," she explained. "Won't you help yourself to punch?"

It didn't look very simple to her, Jess decided as she rushed back into the house. She felt uneasy when she saw that the ladies had left their purses out in the open in the guest bedroom. Well, that wasn't her business where they put them. She noticed, too, that a handsome dark-bearded man in a tuxedo was playing the grand piano in the living room.

Suddenly, it was time to put on the ice water, and the guests were coming to the tables. Jess rushed to the kitchen to pick up the salads, and while the guests ate them, she hurried outside to clean up the plates and punch cups from the patio. Before she knew it, it was time to remove the salad plates and serve the dinner plates of Chicken Cordon Bleu, tiny yellow and green squash, and wild rice. Next, there was sauce to serve, and by then the water glasses were empty.

"Don't spill!" Becky whispered to Jess as they rushed past each other on the way to the kitchen.

"Don't even mention it!" Jess returned.

In the kitchen, Em was already cutting the chocolate cheesecakes for dessert, and Mrs. Wurtzel filled silver coffee servers from the huge coffeemaker. "Fill yer own coffee servers here," she told the girls, "and clear the dinner plates soon as everyone is done eatin'."

Jess crossed her eyes and hurried out to her table again. It felt like a wild race.

Finally, the guests were finishing their dessert and coffee, which meant only one more clean-up before they would begin to wash all the dishes, silverware, glasses, pots and pans.

Mrs. L. came from her place at the head of the dining room table and invited the guests in the entry to join them in the living room for the musicale. "And haven't my young friends, Jess and Becky, done a fine job of serving? They're part of the Twelve Candles Club, a girls' working club that I can recommend most highly."

The guests nodded and smiled at the girls.

"Do you care for more coffee?" Jess inquired, blushing.

After the guests had finished and headed into the living room, Jess and Becky began removing the rest of the dishes from the tables and took them to the kitchen. Before long, the kitchen counters were full of china, crystal, and silver to be washed. Mrs. Wurtzel stored the leftovers, and Em announced, "I'll do the washin'. You girls dry." She was already running water into the sinks. "Compared to some parties, this ain't nothin'."

Jess hated to think of serving more than twenty-four guests for a sit-down dinner. After the goblets and punch cups were dried and put away, she excused herself to use the restroom.

Mrs. Wurtzel eyed her suspiciously. "Well, hurry then, and don't use the powder room. That's fer *them*." She yanked her thumb toward the living room.

A buzz of voices rose over the music from the living room as Jess made her way down the hallway. The guest bedroom door was closed, though. She knocked, but suddenly heard something crash to the floor.

Swallowing hard, Jess called, "Excuse me—"

No one answered.

"Excuse me—" she said again, opening the door slowly.

A man with long, dirty blond hair rushed out through the French doors, his hands full of purses. He'd knocked over a chair—

For an instant Jess stared in shock, then she yelled, "Stop . . . thief! *S-t-o-p, t-h-i-e-f!*"

The music from the living room jerked to a stop, and Mrs. L.'s excited voice floated down the hallway. "Thief? Did someone shout thief?"

Jess's feet felt stuck to the floor for an instant, then shouting "Thief!" again, she dashed after the man through the French doors.

Up the street, she heard a motor sputter to life and tires squeal as a vehicle took off.

Jess ran as fast as she could. As she arrived at the curb, she wasn't too surprised to see the battered blue van again, just before it disappeared around the corner.

When Jess returned to the house, she heard Mrs. Wurtzel's brassy voice above the others. "Wouldn't surprise me none if them girls ain't in cahoots with that robber!"

CHAPTER

9

"Can you believe what Mrs. Wurtzel said?" Jess murmured as she and Becky washed Mrs. Bay's blue Oldsmobile. It was Saturday morning, and they had more cars to wash than ever, with Tricia and Cara out of town.

"Why would she think we were in cahoots with that burglar?" Becky asked, frowning.

Jess shook her head. "Don't ask me! The worst part is, the police might really suspect us. We're going to have to prove that we're innocent!"

Becky swished a wet sponge over the windshield. "You know, when we worked at Mrs. Llewellyn's barbecue, Mrs. Wurtzel didn't seem to like the fact that we were there. Maybe it was the last straw for her when we were hired to work at Mrs. L.'s dinner party, too. A caterer probably makes money on each of the helpers she brings."

"Could be," Jess replied. "Anyhow, it really made me angry when she all but accused us."

Jess could still picture in her mind the police car wailing up to the front door, the two policemen jumping out and questioning everyone, then dusting the guest bedroom for fingerprints. The worst part was that they'd found her prints all over the doorknob.

Later, Mrs. Wurtzel had told the policemen, "Wouldn't surprise me none if them girls ain't in on this with that burglar. Look at them candle medallions they wear 'round their necks," she said. "Probably belong to one of them cults."

Becky glanced up from wringing out her sponge in the soapy water. "You know, Jess, we're going to have to forgive her."

"No way!" Jess shot back. "She was being mean on purpose."

"God wants us to forgive her anyhow."

Jess didn't want to hear it. She slopped a bucket of sudsy water over the car's rear wheel and began to scrub it. After a while, she felt as if someone were watching her, and she looked down at the street. *Mr. and Mrs. Merwich!*

Jess sat down on the ground. "You know," she said, "I wouldn't be surprised if the Merwiches aren't somehow connected to all this trouble. They are always nosing around."

"Now you're as bad as Mrs. Wurtzel," Becky told her.

Jess rose to her knees and polished the hubcap. "I guess so."

"Could be they're taking the Neighborhood Watch more seriously because they're house-sitting," Becky said. "Besides, they're retired and probably don't have much to do in someone else's house. What makes you so suspicious of them?"

"They just look strange to me, always peering around through those owly glasses," Jess said. "Especially him."

Becky ran the squeegee across the windshield. "Just because he wears those thick glasses doesn't mean he's weird. Anyhow, Mom says he has to wear thick glasses because he sees double."

"I'm still not so sure," Jess countered.

After washing nine cars, the girls hurried home for lunch, then met again to clean the Terhunes' house. "Thank goodness I won't have much to do tonight when I baby-sit for the Stallings," Jess said. "Let's hope that dumb burglar keeps his distance!"

———

Just before seven o'clock, Jess passed the Herrington house on her way to the Stallings, and noticed that Mr. and Mrs. Merwich had brought out chairs and were sitting near their front walk. Didn't they know that in this neighborhood people sat on their patios out back?

"Good evening, Jess!" Mrs. Merwich called out to her.

"Hi," Jess answered politely, giving a little wave.

"Have you noticed the Neighborhood Watch signs have already gone up?" Mrs. Merwich asked. "Thanks to your mother's fast work. She's a real organizer."

Jess nodded, wondering if the signs would stop the burglar. Maybe he couldn't even read.

As she walked up the sidewalk to the Stallings' peach two-story house, she noticed it was the same model and color as Tricia's. The Stallings had just moved in a few months ago, and Cara had already warned her that the living room wasn't furnished yet.

Mrs. Stallings, a pretty blond woman, opened the door before Jess knocked. "It's so good of you to sit for us tonight, Jess."

"Ah, Cara says your girls are really nice, so I thought it'd be easy," Jess admitted. "Usually I don't do much baby-sitting."

Mrs. Stallings laughed. "Did you hear that, girls? You have a reputation to keep up in this neighborhood."

Staci, who was six, and Kelli, five, peered around the corner at Jess. They were already in their pajamas, and looked like smaller versions of their mother.

Jess presented Mrs. Stallings with her Baby-sitting Safety Checklist. "I hope you don't mind, but I have to fill this out."

"We already filled out the one Cara gave us and posted it by the phone," Mrs. Stallings said. "We just changed the phone number for where we'll be tonight. Let me show you how the doors and windows lock."

She took Jess around the house, although nothing was much different than at Jess's own house. "We've ordered draperies for the back windows, but they're not here yet. If it bothers you, just turn on the back yardlight."

Jess swallowed hard when she noticed that they had a hill behind their house just like the one behind her own, but it was set back farther. A good place for burglars to case the house.

Mr. Stallings, blond like his wife, lifted each of his daughters high in the air and kissed them. Mrs. Stallings looked pleased, then kissed the girls good-night, too.

Jess could tell they were a happy family.

"There are fresh brownies on the counter and milk in the refrigerator," Mrs. Stallings said to Jess on the way out.

Jess said goodbye and locked the door behind them. "Well, Staci and Kelli, what do you want to do first?"

"Eat brownies!" Staci said. "Then we can read. Cara always reads books to us in our room."

The girls sat down on small chairs at a little white table in the family room, and Jess put a brownie and milk at each of their places. Then she sat on the floor to join them. So far it was fun, she decided.

When they'd finished their snack, Jess said, "Okay, let's go upstairs. Don't choose a book that's too hard for me now!"

They eyed her curiously, then smiled at her joke.

Upstairs, they settled in Staci's room because she had more books. Jess sat down on the floor with them, looking out the back window at the hill. "What book should we read?"

Kelli pulled a picture book out from the back of other books in the bookcase. "This spooky one. It's about wild things."

"You sure?" Jess asked.

They nodded, their blond heads bobbing up and down. "Don't tell Mama we still have it," Kelli said. "She throwed it away, but we got it back from the garbage."

Jess eyed the cover. Wild-eyed monsters with purple hair and creepy-crawly bodies stared back at her. No wonder their mother had thrown it out. "You're sure you want to hear this stuff?"

They both nodded.

Jess read the title aloud. "Darkness Monsters."

The girls' eyes sparkled with excitement, and they leaned over to look at the pages with Jess.

First there were just swirls of bright colors and blackness, and Jess began to read: "Do you know who lives in the darkness? Do you know who lives where there is no light?"

On the next page, jagged shapes with red eyes oozed out of the darkness. "*Monsters*," she read, "gory gnomes and goblins, gremlins and spooky spirits."

Jess slammed the book shut. "Let's read another book.

This one will give you bad dreams. Does Cara read it to you?"

They shook their heads. "No, Cara won't."

Jess stuffed it back into the bookshelf. "Here, let's read about real people. This book looks much better."

By eight o'clock the girls were sleepy, and Jess sent them to the bathroom, then settled them into their beds.

Going downstairs again, Jess was glad it wasn't dark outside yet. She sat down on the brown couch in the family room and zapped on the TV with the remote control. An oldie band with older people dancing flashed on the screen. She tried another channel. A documentary about China; she switched it again. *Mission Impossible*—her most *unfavorite* program. She clicked to the next channel.

Finally—something halfway interesting. A woman was walking along the ocean shore, the wind whipping her long hair around her. Suddenly the music turned spooky and a huge hand came out of nowhere and grabbed the woman. Jess zapped off the TV. Just the kind of movie her brother Jordan would go for. He liked spooky shows, and he especially liked to scare her.

Jess glanced out to the hill. Movement!

Whew! It was only the Herrington's black and white cat.

Still, Jess had a peculiar feeling. She forced herself to get up, walk to the sliding glass door, and flip on the outside light. It lit up a small circle of darkness beyond the house. She could sit at the front of the house, but there was only the kitchen, dining room, and unfurnished living room.

Outside, the night was growing darker, and Jess knew anyone who might be out there could see in. She flicked on the TV again, and the woman by the ocean gave a blood-curdling scream.

Jess's hair tingled on the back of her neck, and she felt creepy all over as she changed the channel to the documentary on China. *At least this isn't scary,* she thought as she tried to concentrate.

Glancing outside again, she saw two red eyes peering in at the glass doors. Her hand flew to her mouth to stifle a scream. It was the cat—just the Herrington's cat.

The phone rang and Jess bolted to her feet. She was sure someone was watching her as she moved like a robot toward the kitchen. On the third ring she picked it up. "Stallings' residence—"

"Grrrmmmpppphhh!" a growl came over the line, followed by a loud click as the creep hung up.

Jess's heart thumped crazily. She pushed in the hang-up button and punched in her home number.

Jordan answered the phone.

"It's me, Jess. I'm baby-sitting at the Stallings', and someone's got to come over here! You know how that Crime Prevention woman said if you feel scared in the pit of your stomach or the hair rises on your neck, something is probably wrong? Well, something's wrong here!"

"Jess, you're crazy!" her brother answered.

"Then let me talk to Dad."

"He and Mom are out," Jordan said.

"Then you or Garn or Mark *please* come," she begged.

"Garn's out on a date, and Mark's gone to bed already."

"Then you come, Jord. Please!"

"No way!" he laughed. "You'll be fine." He hung up.

Jess turned slowly around.

The darkness outside seemed alive with movement. She walked stiff-legged around the breakfast bar and casually turned off the lights to the kitchen and family room. The TV was still on, and Jess lay down on the kitchen floor, shaking. At least no one could see her here, and she could reach the phone if someone broke in.

Never in her life had she felt so absolutely t-e-r-r-i-f-i-e-d.

CHAPTER

10

*H*ow was your baby-sitting job last night?" Jess's dad asked as he drove toward the church. It was only she and Jordan who decided to go with their dad today.

"The baby-sitting job was all right, but being alone in that house was awful," Jess answered from the backseat. "There were no drapes in the family room, and I got one of those growling monster phone calls besides. I was scared stiff. I phoned home for someone to come, but big brother Jordan here just laughed and hung up."

Dad darted a glance at her brother. "How could you do that?"

"She was just being dumb," Jordan scoffed.

Jess leaned forward. "Have I ever before asked you to help me when I was scared? Never ever!"

Her father shook his head. "Jordan, I am disappointed in you. Jess is not a baby. If she says she's frightened, she probably has good reason. If she ever asks you for help again, I expect you to go to her rescue. Especially now, with a burglar loose in the neighborhood. We are a family, and we have to help one another."

Jordan stared straight ahead without a word. It was a good thing, too, because Jess felt like sticking her tongue out at him, or worse—she felt like crying.

Suddenly she suspected it wouldn't do to be angry with him, or the burglar, for that matter. Especially not on her way to church. Tricia and Becky were always talking about forgiveness—even for criminals.

Santa Rosita Community Church was a white Spanish-style building, and lots of people streamed toward the front door.

"Hmmm," Jess's father said, "looks like my old friend, Don Wirt, has quite a turnout on Sundays. I'm not surprised, though, after that men's Bible study the other morning."

Jess tensed up, then remembered something. "Becky and Tricia sure like it here. But they go to Sunday school."

"Would you like to join them?" her dad asked.

"I'll sit with you. I don't know much about this church stuff."

Her father nodded. "Which is why I'm glad both of you agreed to come with me. Jordan, would you like to try the high school group?"

Jordan shook his head. "Not today."

He sounds as uneasy as I feel, Jess thought. *Anyhow, it can't be too bad. Why else would there be so many people here?*

A pretty blond high school girl waved. "Hi, Jord!"

"Jennifer!" he called back through the open car window, then said half to himself, "I didn't know she went here."

"I'm sure all kinds of great kids do," Dad said, maneuvering the car into a parking space. "I heard forty high school kids went on a retreat last weekend."

"Forty?" Jordan marveled.

"Forty," his dad repeated. "Okay, I guess we're all going into the sanctuary—the main part of the building."

Jordan kept his eye on Jennifer, who was heading for the double front doors. "I guess so."

Inside, the church was painted white, too, and organ music filled the big room. An usher handed a bulletin to each of them, and they walked halfway up the aisle to find seats. People looked friendlier than in most places, Jess decided. Maybe it'd be okay. They sat down and she settled back. She glanced at the cover of the bulletin. It was like no other picture she had ever seen of Jesus. He looked strong, almost athletic, nothing like the graceful statues she'd seen at the cemetery gates. The picture seemed to come alive in her hand; His eyes seemed to look into hers. Below were the words, "I can do all things through Christ, which strengtheneth me." The same verse old Elspeth had written in her Bible!

Jess studied the bulletin, thinking that if she read it carefully now, it might prevent her from doing something dumb during the service. Her gaze stopped at, "For God has not given us the spirit of fear, but of power, and of love, and of a sound mind." Tricia had once quoted that verse.

Jess felt more relaxed. At least she knew a little.

Hymnal pages rustled as the organist played the introduction to a new song. Her father found the page and held the hymnbook up so she could share it. At one point everyone stood up, and Jess quickly stood between her dad and Jordan.

The music seemed to float through the church like a brilliant sunrise: "Joyful joyful we adore thee, God of glory, Lord of love; Hearts unfold like flowers before thee, Opening to the sun above . . .

The gray-haired minister was up front singing with the others, and Jess noticed the enormous wooden cross that hung on the white wall behind him. When the song ended, the minister said with a strong voice, "May Christ dwell in your hearts by faith."

There were Bible readings and more songs, and then the minister began to give what the bulletin referred to as the "message." It was all about forgiveness, and Christ dwelling in people's hearts. Jess didn't quite get it. Maybe she should have gone to Sunday school after all.

When the service was over, the three of them made their way out of the church and climbed back into the white Toyota. Jess hadn't seen Becky but looked forward to telling her she had been there.

As soon as they were in the car Jordan turned to Jess. He gulped so hard his Adam's apple bobbed in his throat. "I . . . I have to ask your forgiveness, Jess."

"What for?" she asked in surprise.

"I . . . I'm the one who made those phantom phone calls," he said, gulping again. "I shouldn't have done it. I know that now."

Jess stared at him. "*You?* But why? Why'd you do it?"

He shrugged. "I just wanted to scare you, I guess. And I felt . . . I don't know, an urge to do something mean. But when I heard that sermon . . . it didn't seem like a fun thing anymore—it seemed wrong, and I knew I had to ask your forgiveness."

He really looks sorry, Jess thought. That was different!

"I'm glad you owned up to it, Jordan," Dad said. "What

sometimes seems like a crazy caper, can turn out to be serious. And once you open yourself up to evil, it's hard to get away from it." He turned to Jess. "Do you forgive him?"

Jess nodded. "Yeh. But please don't ever pull another stunt like that again!"

"I won't. I promise."

Looking at her brother, an idea flew into Jess's mind. If God could make Jordan confess, He could probably work things out between her mom and dad, too! Maybe He could even help them catch up with the burglar!

———

Late that afternoon, Cara phoned. "I can come to your slumber party! I've already called the others to remind them to bring their clown suits for the video. See you soon!"

"See you, Cara." Jess grinned as she hung up the phone. *Guess I'd better straighten up my room.*

She quickly made her bed, then grabbed the heap of sweaty gym clothes and dumped them into the clothes hamper. She glanced at the old trunk. Her dad had hung the pictures of Oakley and Elspeth and family above it. Jess thought it added a quaint touch. At her desk, she emptied a bag of chips into a wooden bowl, and opened a can of mixed nuts. She'd already made a huge bowl of popcorn, and her mother said she'd pick up pizza from Morelli's.

Jess threw a worried look at the back window, then hurried over to peer through the slats of the mini-blinds. No one was there—of course. She grabbed the cord, pulling the blind all the way up, and opened the window for fresh air. Anyone could see her family was home because there were cars in the driveway. Besides, Jordan had admitted to making the phantom phone calls. She couldn't get over the fact that her brother had actually asked her forgiveness.

Minutes later she heard her friends. "Order in the court, the monkey wants to speak . . . speak, monkey, speak!"

"Not again!" she wailed as she opened the door.

The three roared with laughter.

"Remember, we *are* Club El Wacko," Tricia said. "Anyhow, we all brought our clown suits, and Cara has the video camera."

"This is going to be just great!" Jess said excitedly as her friends trooped in with their sleeping bags.

"What are we going to do first?" Becky asked.

Jess got her red clown suit and wig from the closet. "Let's do the clown video first, then we'll have pizza. For a change, we don't have to have a business meeting. And guess what? Jordan admitted he'd been making those anonymous phone calls!"

"You're joking!" Cara said, incredulous.

Jess nodded. "Don't tell him I told you. He didn't say it was a secret, but he'd probably die of embarrassment. We went to church this morning, and Jordan started feeling bad about the phone calls, so he asked for my forgiveness."

Tricia and Becky looked at each other, then Tricia said, "Wow! Sounds like major conviction."

"What does that mean?" Jess asked.

"That the Lord was working in Jordan's heart to let him know that the phone calls were wrong," Becky answered.

"I guess so," Jess said. "Anyhow, I'm glad there won't be more of them."

The girls climbed into their clown outfits. "I brought the makeup," Tricia said, "but we don't need to do all of it. Maybe the wigs and red noses are enough."

Jess looked in the big mirror by the back window to adjust her wig. "You know, we do look good," she said, admiring herself. "Even without all the makeup." She stuck on the red foam-rubber nose.

The girls lined up in front of the mirror and laughed hysterically.

"All right!" Cara yelled, getting the video camera. "First, Tricia, you do the intro like we discussed on the way over. Maybe we should do it by the gym equipment. It would give a more interesting background."

Tricia nodded, flopping her yellow wig. "After the intro, Jess, you do some comedy tumbling, and I'll tell about our clown birthday parties. Then I'll take the camera, and Becky and Cara can do the Hokey-Pokey."

"Comedy tumbling?" Jess asked.

"Sure, anything funny," Tricia said.

Jess got up on the balance beam, careful not to trip on her ankle ruffles. "I guess I could try to balance, and then keep falling off . . . then jump onto the trampoline and bounce higher and higher as if I couldn't stop."

"Perfect," Cara said, pointing the camera at her. "Let's try it. We can always do a retake. Everyone ready?"

Standing on the balance beam, Jess fluffed up her red wig and adjusted her baggy clown suit. "Ready!"

Cara called out, "Ready . . . camera . . . action!"

Tricia raised her arms dramatically and jingled her wrist bells. "Introducing the Polka-dot Clowns! I'm Jingles," she said, taking a bow. "And that's Beck-o taking a bow in her blue polka-dot suit." She gestured grandly toward Jess. "And there's our award-winning comedy tumbler, Fireplug!"

Jess took a bow, teetered on the balance beam, then fell off and bounced up and down on the trampoline.

Tricia continued. "Lello is kinda shy, and behind the camera right now. We do birthday parties, picnics, and other programs for kids. Here's a sample." She paused, then said in her ringmaster voice, "Ladies and gentlemen, boys and girls of all ages! Form a circle, and Lello and Beck-o will lead you in dancing the world-famous Hokey-Pokey!"

Tricia took the camera, and Cara and Becky led in the dance. They joined hands. "You put your right foot in, you put your right foot out. . . ."

"For small children, we sing favorite songs like 'Old Mac-Donald,' " Tricia continued, "or others of your choice." Next, she went into her balloon skit, with Becky playing the kids' parts.

Jess climbed back onto the balance beam, waiting for Tricia's cue.

Jingles and Beck-o had just finished the balloon skit when the outside door of Jess's room burst open.

"No one move!" a man shouted, waving a gun and walking unsteadily into the room.

Cara-Lello quickly sat down on the bed and hid the video camera under the pillow behind her.

Jess tottered on the balance beam, then caught her balance as he approached her. It was the burglar all right, the one with the long, dirty blond hair. Jess gulped hard as she realized, *He's only a high school kid!* His eyes were bleary and his speech fuzzy. *He's got to be weirded out on drugs,* she thought.

"You! Stay up there," he growled, then threw a burlap bag at Becky-Beck-o. "Put them silver trophies in the bag. Always did want some of them things. After that, I'll clean out the good stuff from the rest of yer house."

Becky-Beck-o picked up the bag and half-whispered, "They're Jess's trophies."

He waved the gun carelessly. "I don't care whose they are! Just do it!"

Jess clenched her fists, but the rest of her body felt weak. He had her father's plastic pellet gun!

"Those trophies have Jess's name on them," Tricia said, her voice quivering.

"Shut up!" he yelled. "Shut yer mouth and do it!" He looked up at Jess. "Get down from there, *now*. Gotta tie you all up so's I can get the stuff from the rest of yer house."

"Tie us up?" Jess repeated, not budging from the balance beam. It seemed unbelievable that the burglar who'd been scaring them to death all week could be so dumb. Why rob people when they were at home and could give a description of you later? She wasn't sure why she spoke, only that the words came from her mouth. "That plastic pellet gun doesn't work!"

His eyes narrowed, and he pointed it up at the ceiling and pulled the trigger. The gun made a *whooosh*, and a pellet hit the ceiling with a loud bang.

"I fixed it," he bragged.

Even so, he's still dumb, Jess thought. The gun had to be reloaded now. But dumb could also be dangerous, and every muscle of her body felt w-e-a-k.

"Now load them trophies!" he shouted at Becky-Beck-o, waving the pellet gun.

Outside, Jess heard Tumbles yipping.

Tricia-Jingles whispered, "Help us, Jesus!" while the verse roared in Jess's head: *I can do all things through Christ, which strengtheneth me.*

With a sudden burst of strength and courage, Jess jumped from the balance beam, hitting the trampoline with her feet like a jackhammer. Covering her head with her arms, she bounced with all of her might—elbows first—against the burglar.

"Ufff!" he choked as he went down, hitting the gym mat, the pellet gun flying across the room.

"Call 911!" Jess yelled, trying to hold the dazed burglar down. But he was too strong and wrenched himself away.

"Help! *Thief!*" Jess shouted as she raced through the front door after him. "Somebody . . . Help!" Yanking the ankle ruffles of her clown suit up over her knees, Jess ran down the driveway as the man headed for his blue van parked in the street.

Mr. and Mrs. Merwich came racing down the sidewalk. "We called the police as soon as we saw his van!" Mr. Merwich yelled as he ran toward Jess, clutching his glasses in his hand.

The burglar glanced back wild-eyed, then ran right past his van.

"Get him!" Mr. Bay yelled, coming out of his garage waving a leaf rake. Mrs. Bay followed with a broom. "We called the police, and they're on the way!"

Flapping along in their yarn wigs and clown suits, Tricia-Jingles and Becky-Beck-o caught up with Jess, while Cara-Lello ran behind and videotaped the whole scene. Meanwhile Jordan, Garner, Mark, and Dad had joined the chase, with Tumbles Burglar-Catcher McColl behind them, yipping and yapping.

"Stop, thief!" everyone shouted. "Get that kid! Stop him!" Neighbors and dogs were joining in from everywhere, until halfway down the block Jess heard the wail of a police siren.

Everyone held back as the police car bore down on the running burglar in the middle of the street. He glanced back, then turned and raised his hands high in the air. "I give up!" he croaked. "I give up!"

Officers Drane and Salvio climbed out of the patrol car, guns drawn. They handcuffed the burglar and muscled him into the backseat of their car.

"Can't say I blame him for giving up so easily," Officer Drane said, chuckling. "The sight of this crowd would be enough to unnerve anyone."

Jess looked around at the wacko sight. Men and women stood in the street with hoes, brooms, shovels, baseball bats, tennis rackets, and any other household item that could serve as a weapon. They wore everything from robes to dripping wet swimsuits to clown outfits. It wasn't exactly what the Crime Prevention Specialist had advised for a Neighborhood Watch, but they'd all flung themselves into the chase.

"Just look at us," someone laughed, pointing at the four clowns.

"And a clown is videotaping us!" Mr. Bay exclaimed.

People began to chuckle, point, and then laugh at one another.

"Three cheers for the neighborhood!" Tricia yelled, leaping about in her green clown outfit. "Three cheers for the Neighborhood Watch!"

After a few moments, as the crowd calmed down, Officer Drane asked the group around him, "Any actual witnesses to the break-in?"

"The clowns!" Mr. Merwich answered. "All eight of them!"

It was a second before Jess remembered he saw double,

but she wasn't about to correct him and spoil the moment.

She looked at Cara-Lello, Becky-Beck-o, and Tricia-Jingles, who were all grinning. "We did it! We really got him!"

"But it wasn't just us clowns and the neighbors," Becky said. "I prayed like anything."

"I did, too," Tricia added. "God works in all kinds of ways!"

Jess remembered how weak she'd felt before she jumped at the robber. She also remembered Tricia saying, "Help us, Jesus!" Then the verse had come to her: *I can do all things through Christ, which strengtheneth me.* Her weakness had vanished, and she'd felt that sudden burst of power before she'd jackhammered onto the trampoline. Power . . . that's exactly what it'd been.

"You're right!" she exclaimed, suddenly not caring what anyone thought. "You're really right about Jesus making a difference!"

More than that, Jessica Elspeth McColl was from this moment determined to be more like that old Elspeth. She was going to do her very best to learn everything she could about Jesus Christ.

Absolutely everything!